PRAISE FOR

"Steamy, romantic, exh....... ......y ...... y ....
mouthwatering story was delivered just right, penned to
perfection, and kept me hypnotized cover to cover."
-Natasha is a Book Junkie

"Undeniably explosive, flirty, and addictive... We were hooked!"
-The Rock Stars of Romance

"Get ready to be hot and bothered because Nikki Sloane creates
the perfect erotic storm and you will love getting caught up in it!"
-Agents of Romance

"Hot, sexy, steamy, and so much more, Nikki delivers a story that
will keep you begging for more!"
-Bella from PBC

"A love story with a side of sexy-as-sin foreplay, erotic exploration,
and characters who know how to excite and pleasure. A scorching
hot read!"
-Roxy Sloane, *USA Today Bestselling Author*

"A slick, captivating, and incredibly sexy book. Sloane injects
humor and depth into a compelling story, and ensures readers
will be back for more."
-SM Book Obsessions

"Three Simple Rules is a smoking hot read that will have you
hooked from the first page. Nikki Sloane is a hot new erotic
author to watch for."
-The SubClub Books

ONE *more* RULE

NIKKI SLOANE

Text copyright © 2015 by Nikki Sloane

All rights reserved. Except as permitted under the U.S. Copyright Act of 1976, no part of this publication may be reproduced, distributed, or transmitted in any form or by any means, or stored in a database or retrieval system, without the prior written permission of the publisher.

The characters and events portrayed in this book are fictitious. Any similarity to real persons, living or dead, is coincidental and not intended by the author.

All Night Long Edition
ISBN 978-1-517-34140-4

for my nymphs

Chapter ONE

PAYTON

Dominic's arm wrapped around my waist, steadying me as the train rocketed around a corner. He clung with one hand to the gray strap overhead, while I used my knees to keep our bags from tumbling over. His luggage slammed painfully into my thigh. The anxiety-inducing thirteen-hour flight from Tokyo had gotten to me.

"I hate riding the El," I said, "when I own an expensive and fucking beautiful car."

Dominic gave a tight smile. "Which is downtown and doesn't have room for your luggage."

"Sure it does. There just wouldn't be room for you."

His fingers flicked me playfully just inside of my hipbone, where the tattoo rested beneath my jeans. He did it whenever I made a joke about our relationship, his wordless reminder of how much I really loved him.

"You better watch it."

"Or what?" I had my hand on his chest and drummed my fingers, challenging his seduction right back.

His embrace tightened further, and his mouth was right by my ear. "Didn't you tell me once you wanted to reenact the scene from Risky Business?"

My face warmed with a smile. I'd suggested that almost a year ago on a Japanese train, but it felt like a lifetime now. Dominic had turned down my offer, worried he'd lose his riding privileges, and I'd learned during my year in Tokyo just how important those were.

Now we were on an elevated train barreling for downtown Chicago, just like the movie.

Well, not exactly. It was midafternoon, and the car was packed, standing room only. I glanced at the bored faces of the travelers around us and shrugged. "I'm game if you are."

"Fuck, Payton, you'd love that, wouldn't you?" His infectious laugh sounded so good, I'd never grow tired of listening to it.

The city we would call home again in three months loomed in the distance. Chicago. Dark, dirty, loud, and everything I wanted. I'd missed the gorgeous skyline, and from Dominic's expression, I could tell he had too.

Once we hit the loop, we got off, lugged our bags down the steps, and headed out onto the sidewalk.

"It feels like we've been gone for years," I said, glancing down the street.

It had been February when Dominic had flown across the world, determined for us to be together, no matter what. Going back to Japan with him was a choice I'd made even before he proposed. Now it was September, and our best friends were getting married.

"Which way is the lake?" I said, exhausted and disoriented. "Did they move it while we were gone?"

"I don't think so." Dominic motioned toward the left.

"Are you guessing, or do you know?" I was giving him attitude when I didn't mean to be. "Fuck, I'm tired."

His expression was amused. "It's four blocks this way, devil woman. I looked it up while we were at baggage claim waiting for the suitcases."

All of our time together, and I still wasn't accustomed to

ONE *more* RULE

his planning. I liked flying by the seat of my pants, making split decisions. Dominic enjoyed thinking ahead.

My suitcase wheels rattled over a grate as I followed beside him. "You love this."

"Having a clue? Yeah."

We hit the lobby of the Opulent Hotel right at three, so we could check in, and I sighed against him during the elevator ride up to our room. "What's the plan again?"

"We'll take a nap to get over some of the jet lag, then meet Evie and Logan for dinner."

"Evelyn," I corrected. It was an inside joke now. He had every right to call her by the nickname, but I loved to tease. The lit floor numbers ticked by as we climbed, bringing us closer and closer to sleep. I could hardly keep my eyes open. "Where are we meeting them?"

"Benihana."

The Japanese restaurant? I'd sell my Jaguar F-Type just for some American food. "Fuck off, we are not."

Dominic's smirk at his joke almost melted my panties. "You're so sexy when you're pissed."

The elevator doors peeled open, and we trekked along the carpet until he had the room door open for me. No need to bother with the lights. Luggage was left by the closet as I went to the curtains and dragged them closed. I tugged off my shirt and tossed it on the chair in the corner, then stripped out of my jeans.

I locked eyes with my fiancé across the room as he began to shed his clothes. A triumphant smile quirked on his lips.

"What?" Was I acting strange? He was looking at me like I was hilarious, when all I was doing was getting ready for was a coma.

"Nothing." His rough voice cut through the darkened room. "Just thinking about the last time we were in a hotel, trying to get some sleep during the day."

I was pulling the cover off and froze mid-action.

"You fought me about getting into bed together," he added. His pants fell off his hips, leaving him in only his boxers, and he came to me, brushing my hair off my shoulder.

"Yeah," I said in a hushed voice. "Last time, I wanted to fuck you, not sleep with you."

His lips skimmed over the curve of my neck, drawing a shudder from my body. "Not true now?"

He loved holding that over me, just one of the many battles he'd won. I couldn't sleep without him now. And yes, I was tired. Two seconds ago my answer would have been I'd rather sleep than screw. But Dominic's touch lit me up and made me burn. "I always want you, Dominic, even after we've been up for nineteen hours."

His lips sealed over mine, and hands tangled in the straps of my bra, tugging them down. The smooth skin of his chest pressed against mine as his arms encased me. Kissing him was insane. When his tongue filled my mouth, I moved mine against it, moaning into the kiss.

"Well," he said, ending it abruptly, "calm down. I need to sleep."

A fucking bluff. My gaze dropped to his boxers, which were tented. I shrugged and faked indifference. "You don't need to be awake for this. I can get what I need."

A startled cry tore from my throat as he tossed me sideways onto the bed, bent over me, and pressed the length of his cock against my center. Only our underwear held us

ONE *more* RULE

back.

"Is this what you need?" The gravel of his voice was more pronounced when he whispered.

I clawed at him, my nails digging in. "Yes."

Dominic slid down my body, his hot mouth coursing a line over my belly. "So, my tongue couldn't get the job done?" He worked lower and lower, tugging the crotch of my panties to the side.

"It can get the job started," I whispered. Cool air wafted over my exposed flesh, but only intensified the ache for him.

He hovered, teasing kisses and touches on the inside of my thighs. Fuck, I needed his mouth on me. This last week, he'd had to work late every night. A drawer full of vibrators didn't compare to my man. I pushed a hand into his soft, fawn-colored hair, urging him to taste me with his wicked tongue.

"What do you want?" he whispered against my skin.

"Fuck me with your mouth."

Bliss rolled up my legs as Dominic's tongue licked over my clit. I had one hand in his hair and the other on the sheet beneath me, and both clenched into fists. My lungs squeezed as a finger plunged inside, taking my pleasure up another level.

He knew exactly how I liked it, but didn't give it to me. His slowly thrusting finger was just a little too gentle, his tongue too hesitant. Teasing. Holding me exactly where he wanted me, right at the edge.

I grew lightheaded and scored my nails over his scalp, desperate for more. He could hear my whimper, begging him without words, but he ignored it. He wanted me to come at his pace, and Dominic was used to getting his way.

I endured his deliberate mouth for a lifetime.

Once my legs began to shake, he kicked into a new gear, flooring my accelerator. His urgent sucking, licking, biting... Two fingers speared into me, filling and stretching in an ache that burned so good. I was about to come, just as he wanted.

"God, please," I moaned, shivering as the waves of the orgasm built.

"Zutto issho ni itai," he said in Japanese. "I want to be with you forever."

I cried out, a strangled sound that died as I burst open. My quivering thighs locked around his head. Oh God, it was good. He was so perfect, from his stunning blue eyes to his desire to give me exactly what I needed. Liquid heat flamed through me, leaving warmth behind.

My legs went boneless as panties were yanked down. Dominic stood, and before I could catch my breath, his hands scooped beneath my knees and pulled me to the edge of the bed, sliding me across the sheets. I clutched at his hips when his thick cock sank into me.

"Yes," I breathed. "I love you."

My left hand walked up his chest, and my engagement ring glinted in the sunlight the hotel curtains couldn't block. I rose up on an elbow, and my grip curled around the back of his neck. I needed him closer, his lips on mine.

His first slow thrust was deep and my toes tensed into points. I arched my back as I pulled his face down, slamming our lips together. Connecting with the love of my life on all levels. His hardened chest flattened against mine, pushing my breasts into him as his thrusts increased in intensity.

"I love you," he whispered, raining kisses along my

ONE *more* RULE

jawline. "Real."

It didn't take long for his tempo to erase my mind and burn away all my exhaustion. My only desire was for him to reach the same climax he'd already given me. Not like it mattered. He wouldn't settle for just one orgasm from my body. He'd go until he had me screaming, and only then would he worry about himself.

"Goddamnit," he groaned, watching me writhe beneath him. I palmed my breast with my right hand, rolling and pinching the nipple between my fingers, and Dominic's pupils dilated with lust. "So fucking hot."

"You're gonna make me come again."

"Good." Hips beat into mine, his cock growing harder as the volume of my moans increased.

"But, shit, you make it impossible to be quiet."

The sapphire eyes gleamed. "Who said you had to be quiet? I know I sure as hell didn't."

"We're . . . in a hotel." It was a challenge not to pant it out.

"And?" He ground his pelvis against my clit, and flashes of electricity danced up my spine.

"People will think you're murdering me again."

His perfect smile spread across his face. "I'm still hazy about that. Did they think I was killing you with my cock? Yeah, you were screaming about it, but how—"

I lifted up on my elbows again and latched my teeth on the side of his neck, drawing a sharp noise of surprise, laced with an edge of pain. It flipped a switch in him. Sweet, playful Dominic went away, replaced by the darker, aggressive version.

"That's how it's going to be?" he asked in his rough

voice. "All right, let me help you be quiet, slut."

He bolted upright, drawing out of me, and the sudden emptiness was shocking. I blinked up at him. Was he really going to stop just because I'd nipped at his neck? I hadn't even left a mark. In fact, I'd never left a mark on him, other than the tattoo on his hip, which had been his idea. He'd marked me plenty of times, not that I was complaining. We both knew how much that turned me on.

When I sat up, chasing after him, a hand gripped my shoulder and pushed me to turn around.

"On your back," he ordered. "Head hanging off the edge of the bed."

I shivered with excitement. I loved his dominant side, which had expanded under Akira's masterful teaching. I scrambled in my eagerness to follow his command, pivoting on my ass and scooting down to lie flat on the mattress.

"Open your mouth so I can fuck it."

My pussy clenched at his dirty words. I barely got my lips open and he was there, sliding his dick inside, wet with my own taste. At this angle, he could drive deep into my throat. I swirled my tongue over him, getting him to pulse, and there wasn't anything else like that sensation. Knowing how much he enjoyed what I was doing to him. I wrapped one hand around his cock, twisting my fist around him as he thrust in and out.

My other hand trailed down between my legs where I was needy and unsatisfied. And no sooner had I started playing with myself than he leaned over me, seized my wrist, and pushed it away.

"No, no, no," he teased. "We don't want you getting too loud."

ONE *more* RULE

I wanted to remind him that he had my mouth occupied, but he dropped my hand at my breast, squeezing down on it.

"You can play with these," Dominic said, dragging our hands over my tits. "But this," his fingers glided down through my wet pussy and slapped my sensitive flesh, "this is fucking mine."

His other hand was a fist, and he set it beside my hip, so he had leverage as he leaned over and sawed his cock in my greedy mouth, slow enough to not gag me. When I tightened my grip, he groaned in approval, and the fingers on my clit rubbed faster. I bucked under his skilled touch.

Compatible wasn't a strong enough word for us. It wasn't like every time we had sex it was the most amazing rapture ever. But we always clicked. Always worked together. Even our mediocre sex was fun and enjoyable. I hoped I'd never take a minute of him for granted.

A rough finger shoved inside me, and I moaned while he was lodged in my throat. "Mmm . . ."

"Fuck." It came out strained. The vibration of my moan must have felt pretty damn good, judging by his reaction. The heel of his palm pressed against my clit while the finger fucked me in time with his hips. Pleasure built at the base of my spine, teasing the orgasm again.

I pumped my fist on him. Used suction. Spun the edge of my tongue on the head of his dick. Everything in my arsenal to bring him to the brink, as he was about to tip me over into ecstasy.

"Shit. Oh, fuck, yes," Dominic said between deep breaths. "Take it."

It was the last push I needed to release, and I exploded. My cries were muffled by his enormous, throbbing cock, and as I came, my legs trembling, it was the wordless permission he needed.

Breath left him in a loud burst, and his movements became jerky and erratic, followed by a long noise of satisfaction, which rumbled up from deep in his chest. He came in spurts, wave after wave, filling my mouth, and when he ceased, I swallowed. It drew another low moan from him.

"Payton," he whispered, his knuckles brushing over my cheekbone. He stepped back and helped me sit up. In a heartbeat, he was seated beside me on the bed, his arms trapping me. I tilted my head so he could trace kisses along my neck, my eyes falling shut and my fingertips gritting over his unshaven face.

His kisses slowed, and reality returned, one layer after another. I blinked sluggishly. We collapsed on the bed and Dominic tugged the sheet up over our sweat-dampened bodies.

A chuckle rang out when I curled up beside him, needing the contact against his warm body. I sighed dramatically, but since he couldn't see my face, I grinned. We'd pushed each other into new territory. Talking. Sleeping in the same bed. Love.

Soon, marriage.

"Hey." I rolled over onto my other hip, turning to face him. "Let's get married."

His eyes were already closed, one hand tucked under his pillow. "Thought we already agreed on that."

"No," I said. "Let's get married while we're home. Tomorrow."

Chapter TWO

Dominic's eyes flew open and a scowl darkened his face. "What?"

As the idea began to take shape, I grew more excited. "We've been living together for a year. The paperwork with our work visas is a pain in the ass. We could go to the courthouse and do one of those quickie Justice of the Peace things."

His face was stoic, but the muscles beneath his jaw tensed, as if clenching his teeth. He wasn't a fan of this idea.

"Have you ever been to any of the Cook County courthouses?" He asked it in a lazy voice, but there was tension beneath. "Because if you had, I don't think you'd be chomping at the bit to go back."

"Okay, the courthouse isn't great, but it's not that bad. Think about it—"

His expression turned serious. "I already have."

I hesitated as the words sank in. He'd considered getting married while we were home, but decided against it. "And . . . ?"

"This is Evie and Logan's wedding, not ours."

"Seriously? We don't even have to tell anyone. Just you and me." My fingers brushed over his jaw, cupping his face. "I'm tired of waiting, and I don't need the big party or the dress. I want to be your wife."

He blinked slowly, and I saw the thought run through his gorgeous eyes. He wanted this too, and badly, but he shook his head. "I really fucking want that, but there are a bunch of reasons why we should wait."

"Yeah?" I deflated somewhat. "Convince me this isn't the best idea ever."

"Our families won't like it."

I raised an eyebrow. Of course it mattered what Dominic's family thought, because they were warm and fuzzy, and the way a family was supposed to be. Besides his sweet parents, I was getting two hilarious sisters-in-law in the deal. I was less interested in what my family had to say about any decision I made in my life.

"I know your family might not like it," I said, "but they'll get over it. I have zero fucks to give about my family."

They'd met Dominic only once, via Skype, in a super awkward ten-minute conversation. That was all the time my selfish parents could spare for the man who wanted to marry their only daughter. Dominic and I had booked our plane tickets months ago for Evie's wedding, in the same fucking city where my parents lived, and still, plans to meet face-to-face were up in the air. I'd sort of stopped trying to make it happen, and I'd bet on my life that we'd fly back to Tokyo without seeing them. "Sorry, Payton, I wish we could, but it's been such a hectic week," I could already hear my mother saying.

"Next," I demanded.

"Your parents said they'd pay for the wedding."

I practically snorted. "See, we'd be saving them money."

He ran a hand over my hip, then fingertips traced in the hollow of my back. "You could invite everyone from the club." The way he delivered the statement was odd. There was some sort of meaning I wasn't picking up on, and his expression turned devious. "I thought you'd love that, your ultra conservative parents footing the bill for dinner and an open bar for a bunch of high-class escorts."

"Oh my God." I couldn't stop the grin. "You're right, I do love that. Fuck, I'm such a bitch." And I wasn't even sorry about it.

"Don't get me wrong, devil woman." The fingertips skimmed up over my shoulder blades, all the way until he tucked a lock of hair behind my ear and cupped my face. "You know I want to give you whatever you want, and I'm so fucking glad that happens to include my last name. But I think I want the party, and the dress, and all that shit. I want everyone there to celebrate with us, and see how incredibly lucky I am."

I felt warm and giddy inside, but I couldn't let on how much his words affected me. Whenever things grew serious, my immediate response was sarcasm to cover my vulnerability. So I faked disdain. "You're such a romantic."

"And maybe I just want a wedding so afterward I can tear the dress off of my wife on our wedding night and fuck her like the dirty girl she is."

I closed the space between us, kissing him sweetly. "Shit, Dominic, you should have led with that. If that's what you want, that's what I want, too."

The alarm on Dominic's phone began chiming at seven, and we stumbled to the shower together, bleary-eyed. Even though it was nine in the morning tomorrow in Japan, the three-hour nap hadn't done much to recharge.

"I saw a Walgreens a block away," Dominic said as he scrubbed shampoo into his hair. "We can grab some Red Bull and slam it in the cab on our way to the restaurant."

"Can I mainline it?"

We hurried to get dressed. Dominic pulled on a French blue button-down shirt with the sleeves rolled back and black pants. The shirt matched the color of his eyes and showed off the watch I'd bought him.

I tugged the hem down of my seafoam green dress and slipped my feet into a sexy pair of nude heels. Then I donned my chandelier earrings and tousled my hair once more. "You ready?"

"I'm waiting for you to ask me something."

What . . . ? Oh. I loved this game. How the fuck had I forgotten? I strolled over to him, hooking my fingers through his belt loops and pulling his lower body tight against mine. "Do I have your permission to wear panties tonight . . . Sir?"

His expression was victory mixed with desire. "I'll allow it for now." His kiss was hungry and over too soon. "You look beautiful tonight," he whispered.

His compliment threw me off balance, but in a great way. I struggled to recover and cracked the joke, "I always look beautiful."

"That's what I love most about you."

"How humble I am?"

It came out serious. "No, that you look almost as good as I do. Your personality's not important."

I flicked him on his hip, hitting his tattoo that matched mine.

ONE *more* RULE

We did exactly as Dominic had suggested and drank Red Bull on our way to the Italian restaurant, which was packed with people. I clung to his thick arm as we wove through the crowd and headed up the stairs to where Logan had texted us the table was located.

Evie looked flat out gorgeous. A pre-wedding glow, perhaps. Her excitement at marrying Logan was like a filter, making everything seem brighter and better. Would I be like this the final days before marrying Dominic? I already felt that way.

I hugged her fiercely. "Fuck, I missed you."

She smiled as she pulled back. "Right back at you."

We turned to watch our fiancés shake hands, which seemed too formal, but I had the feeling Logan wasn't the hugging type. Which was exactly why I stepped up and wrapped my arms around him. He went rigid in my embrace and his gaze shifted to Dominic, worried. It made me choke back a laugh. Yeah, I'd had sex with Logan, but I knew Dominic was comfortable with this. I'd made it crystal clear to my future husband that he was all I ever wanted. And it was so much fun to see typically composed Logan uncomfortable.

I squeezed a hand on Logan's shoulder. "You remember what I said?"

"That if I'm late to the wedding, you'll rip off my dick and shove it up my ass?" Logan's intense eyes blinked, unfazed. "No, I'd forgotten. Please tell me again."

"If anyone's going to be late," Evie said, "I think we know who that'll be." She gestured to herself.

Logan gave me a serious look. "I'm counting on you to get her there on time. She has this way of making you think she's on schedule, and then drops the bomb ten minutes before departure that she wants to take a quick shower."

Evie snorted. "One time, Logan. And why, exactly, did I need the shower?"

Logan's gaze drifted up to the left as he recalled the memory, and a half-smile bowed on his lips. He tugged her close to him and whispered something. It was hard to hear in the noisy restaurant, but sounded like, "Because you were dirty."

We sat, ordered drinks, and chitchatted about random things. Our flight, their jobs, the wedding. Dominic's arm rested comfortably on the back of my chair, his thumb brushing patterns on my shoulder.

Evie wore a sleeveless black dress that draped in the front and hung low to give a peek at her cleavage. She was a beautiful woman, and although Logan was attractive, he was lucky to have her. Evie fucking rocked. When I'd quit my job at Rosso Media Group and began working at the club, she hadn't judged me. Nor did she abandoned me, or try to talk me out of it as some of my other friends had. Evie got me.

And that was probably what I liked most about Logan. He treated her as if she were everything, even with the way he looked at her. She was the center of his goddamn universe. My final night as a working girl at the club, I'd been on the table wishing I could find a connection to someone just a fraction as strong as what they had.

In walked Dominic, and boom. Done.

The conversation floated from topic to topic easily, like no time had passed with us being apart. There was a pang in my stomach. I already knew I'd spend my first week back in Tokyo being fucking homesick. Just three more months.

ONE more RULE

"What are the plans tonight?" Evie asked, her attention focused on me. "Or do we not get to know them?"

An evil grin warmed my face, and beneath the table, I squeezed Dominic's knee. We spoke at the same time. "It's a surprise."

I dug into my purse, pulled out the tiara I'd bought, and set it on the table. It was decorated with plastic penises, and everyone stared at it, the peach colored cocks on springs waving comically.

"Don't worry, Logan," Dominic deadpanned. "That's for Evie."

"Evelyn," I corrected, but Dominic just smirked.

Logan raised an eyebrow and his attention swung to his fiancé, his voice teasing. "Still remember what they look like?"

Evie's face flushed as she clenched the tiara in her hand and set it in her lap, hiding it from view. "Ha, ha, boss."

Well, that was weird. "What do you mean?"

"Nothing, don't worry about it." My friend's voice was high and rushed. Apparently she hadn't gotten any better at lying since I'd left Chicago.

"Oh, no. Tell me, or you put the Princess Penis crown on right now."

The men chuckled, but I was entirely serious, and it was obvious from Evie's nervous look she knew. A deep breath was sucked in. She tucked a lock of hair behind an ear, straightened her shoulders, and gave me a plain look.

"I told Logan no more sex before the wedding."

Chapter THREE

For a moment, sound fell from the room. I couldn't focus my thoughts. "What the fuck? Why?"

"Because," she snapped, "I want our wedding night to be special, okay? I liked the idea of building the anticipation, and I thought no sex or nudity would do that."

"Shit, no nudity either?" Dominic's voice was thinly veiled horror. Was he worried I'd like this concept and want to do something similar? It sounded like fucking torture.

Logan had a pained smile, as if it were humorous and awful at the same time. "Yeah. She changes in our bathroom or the closet with the door shut."

"When did the rule go into effect?" I asked Evie, who stared at her shrimp appetizer.

There was no hesitation from Logan. "Thirty seven days ago."

Oh. My. God. Dominic and I exchanged glances. How was this going to affect our plans?

Her voice was soft. "I didn't make the rule to punish us."

Logan shifted in his seat, leaning into her as he radiated concern. "Hey, I know that. I . . . I don't know if like is the right word, but I understand the rule. You know I won't break it." His fingers curled under her chin and tilted her up into a soft kiss. "I did think you'd cave by now, though, naughty girl. You hardly ever follow the rules."

Their intimate moment forced me to turn to Dominic.

ONE *more* RULE

"No sex for thirty-seven days. I might die."

He scowled. "That's nothing. Try going a fucking year."

I pressed my lips together to hold back the giggle. He'd gone that long without sex when he'd first moved to Japan, before we met. "Oh, yeah. Poor Dominic. We made up for lost time, though."

"We're still making up for it. There are at least a dozen inches in our apartment where I haven't fucked you yet."

"It's so spacious," I said of our microscopic place. "I don't know how we'll get it done in the next three months."

Our server delivered our dinners, and once she was gone, I went needling for clarification. "The no nudity rule only applies to you two, right?"

Logan glanced to Evie, probably trying to conceal his hopefulness.

"Yeah," she said. "If Dominic wants to take Logan to a strip club, that's—"

I giggled. "Slut, I wasn't asking for him."

We finished dinner, and although Evie pried for more information, Dominic and I stayed tight-lipped. He received the text message we were waiting for just a few minutes after he'd paid the bill, and we escorted the bride and groom toward the lobby.

"You drive?" Dominic's question was directed to Logan.

"No, is that a problem?"

I shook my head as I pushed through the front door. "Nope, it's perfect." I strolled toward the black stretch limo that was pulled up out front, and enjoyed the curious looks of the people on the sidewalk.

The stout driver wore a black suit and a friendly smile. "Mrs. Ward?"

I grinned. "Yeah, someday. Are you Saul?" When he nodded, I added, "Awesome. Hope you're ready for a wild night."

Saul smoothed a hand over his dark hair and flashed an easy smile. "Whatever you say, ma'am."

"You got a limo?" Evie's eyes were wide, scanning the length of black tinted windows.

"Fuck yeah, we did," I said. Saul hurried to open the back door, and I gestured to my best friend. "In you go." She ducked inside, and I glanced at Logan. "Now you, Stone."

Logan's dark eyes narrowed the slightest bit before he followed her. Yeah, he didn't like being bossed around, and he probably didn't like being in the dark about the plans. I stifled my chuckle. He was about to be a whole lot more in the dark.

I climbed in, sliding across the back bench and Dominic's impressive form was beside me a moment later, seated on the black leather. The ceiling was lit with silver LED lights, which sparkled and winked like stars. Logan and Evie were perched on the side bench, facing the bar where a bottle of champagne was holstered in the ice bucket.

"You guys didn't have to do this," she said, playing it cool, but I could tell how much this meant to her, and I was thrilled. She deserved it.

And even though it was Dominic's money that was paying for the night, I'd helped him plan. This limo had been my suggestion, as had been our first stop, so I dug into my purse and found what I was looking for.

Dominic reached for the champagne when the limo eased its way into traffic. "Of course we did," he said. "It's not every day Logan decides to get married." His gravel voice had an upswing of teasing to it, then dipped back into serious territory. "I didn't think he'd ever get hitched, but obviously he was waiting for you."

A warm expression flitted through Evie's eyes as my fiancé popped the cork on the bottle with a dull thump. Logan looked pleased, grabbed a crystal tumbler off the bar, and held it ready. Golden champagne was poured. The glass was passed to Evie, and as soon as it was done, I tore open the plastic wrap in my hands and handed her something else.

Her blue eyes scanned the black blindfold and she licked her lips. Was it in anxiety or excitement? Or was she thinking about the last time I'd handed her a blindfold, and the scorching hot threesome that had ensued? Her fingers brushed mine as she took it. It was impossible not to think about, but it had to be worse for her. She was the one who'd gone more than a month without sex.

"And for you, Logan." I tugged open the second wrapper and held it out for him.

He stared at the blindfold as if wary, and his gaze flicked to Dominic, who shrugged like he had no idea what was going to happen, even though he did.

The soon-to-be newlyweds locked gazes, communicating through a wordless conversation. Evie let out a breath, then slipped the blindfold on, tugging it over her closed eyes. Logan hesitated, but Dominic's indifferent attitude while he continued to pour drinks seemed to do the trick.

"I feel like a fucking idiot," Logan said when he had it over his eyes.

"Well, you look great," Dominic joked. "And don't worry, Payton and I aren't going to get naked and fuck or anything now." Even under the blindfold, Logan didn't seem thrilled. "I'm handing you your champagne—"

A hand reached for it at the exact moment Dominic moved, knocking the glass and champagne sloshed over the side, splashing Logan.

"Fuck, watch it." Dominic's voice was amused. He used his other hand to guide Logan's to the glass.

"It would be easier if I could see."

"Where's the fun in that?" I said.

It was a short ride to the Baton Lounge, but probably felt longer to Evie and Logan. After the initial uncomfortable moments wore off, it seemed to relax both of them. Like it did to me, putting a restriction on them made them feel more open. No pressure to do anything. Just sit back, I thought, and let me and Dominic take charge.

Maneuvering them out of the limo while they were still wearing the blindfolds was fun. As Evie stood on the sidewalk, I set the crown of cocks on her head, working to get it to sit right.

"Yeah," she said. "Make sure it's on straight, because it would be so embarrassing if it was crooked."

I looped my arm through hers and urged her forward, keeping her from stumbling as we went in through the open door. There was a loud bang, a noise of pain, and I turned to see Logan backing away, as if he'd run into the pane of glass beside the entrance.

"Oh," Dominic said. "Watch out, there's a door ahead." He grinned, clearly enjoying busting Logan's balls.

"What the hell, Dominic?" Logan demanded.

Evie's face contorted with worry. "Are you okay?"

"He's fine," I said.

It was muttered by Logan, but still loud enough for me to hear. "Asshole." His hands searched, then grasped a shoulder, letting Dominic guide him.

The large room had tiered seating with tables, and a stage along the back wall. The woman just inside the door scanned the tickets on my phone, and didn't seem to care about Evie's tiara or blindfold. She did, however, stare at Dominic like he was naked. It was both annoying and kind of an ego boost. This stranger lusted after him, and could I really fault her for that? That night I'd met Dominic, I'd thought he was crazy good-looking, and time only made him hotter.

"You're in the front row," she said, her glittering eyes never leaving him. "Your server can help you find the table."

Like it was really that hard.

We had our friends seated at the table and ordered drinks before we let them take off their blindfolds. "Give them back to me," I said over the din of the crowd. "This is just our first stop."

"Where are we?" Logan glanced around, evaluating his surroundings. "And why are Dominic and I the only guys here?"

He was right, the audience was ninety-nine percent female. I laughed. "Trust me, you're not the only guys here."

It was at that precise moment the plus-sized host took the stage, wearing a sparkling blue dress and a heavy coat of makeup. She strolled up to the microphone, brushed her long dark red hair over her shoulder, and gave us a sexy look.

"Good evening, ladies. I'm your host, Ginger."

If the glitzy dress and overdone makeup hadn't already done it, the deep voice was what clued Logan in.

"Is that a—"

"Drag queen?" Dominic answered. "Oh, yeah."

Logan's gaze bounced between the performer on stage, to Dominic, and back again. He had to be wondering what the hell they were doing here.

"I made a deal with Dominic," I said. "We stick together tonight. This is what I wanted for Evie, and we'll get to yours later. Sorry."

The truth was I trusted Dominic, and hell, I trusted Logan too, to keep their dicks in their pants during their bachelor party. But who I didn't trust, was other people. I'd had bachelor parties come through the blindfold club, and I'd seen things escalate beyond what anyone intended. Plus, the girl drooling over Dominic when we first walked in only affirmed my decision. It would be easier for him to brush off any unwanted attention if I was right beside him.

The show began. It was one female impersonator's set right after another. Gorgeous dresses, fake tits, and tuck jobs that were fucking magic. They danced, lip-synced to Lady Gaga and Whitney Houston, and took tips from the female audience, who treated them to catcalls and cheers. The show was a riot.

Our men sat, transfixed. Curious, but trying not to display it.

"Holy shit." It came from Evie when a blonde stepped on stage in five-inch heels and a mini-skirt. "He has nicer legs than I do."

By the time the final number was over, we were all buzzing from our drinks, and uptight, control freak Logan sort of looked relaxed. Perhaps it was Evie's hand resting high on his thigh, lingering close to the danger zone.

ONE *more* RULE

After we filed out of the Baton Lounge, we mobbed with the rest of the crowd in the warm September night, and strolled slowly down the block to where our limo waited. We ducked inside one by one.

"That was awful," Dominic said, a smile twisting on his sexy lips. "The ones that were obviously dudes were fine, but the other ones..."

I giggled. "Your dick get confused?"

His arm hooked around my shoulders and pulled me close. "Be quiet, devil woman."

"Or?"

"Spankings." His lip curled in a half-smile.

I played up my eagerness by batted my eyelashes. "Now?"

"Well, we'll get their blindfolds back on first."

"Oh, of course."

Our friends stared at us like they were unsure if we were serious. I knew Dominic wasn't, but if he wanted to... he certainly knew I was game. Instead, I retrieved the blindfolds and passed them out.

Logan looked even less excited about it this time around. "Calm down." I motioned for him to put it on. "The only queen for the rest of the night is the one wearing the cock crown."

His head swung toward Evie. "It does look great on you."

"Thanks, boss. Should I wear it to work on Monday?"

"Sure. That wouldn't be an HR nightmare."

They put their masks on at the same time, and like me, Evie curled up under her fiancé's arm, snuggling close, one hand on Logan's chest. His fingers stroked up and down her bare arm. She tucked in further, putting her lips against his neck.

The gentle, sweet kiss she'd started grew when he turned his head into hers, bringing their mouths together. It was like she'd struck a match and set Logan on fire, and although it was probably weird as hell for me to watch our friends making out, I did it anyway. I'd spent more than a year at the club and had seen every sexual act done in a wide range of ways. But the way Evie's needy hands clutched at his shirt while he devoured her kiss was so fucking sexy.

His hands reached out, finding her hips, and then he pulled her into his lap so she was straddling him. The skirt of her dress rode up on her thighs, and Dominic's gaze automatically turned out the window.

"Such a gentleman," I whispered to him, knowing he was probably blushing. Just another thing I loved about him.

A soft sigh came from Evie, drawing my attention back to the couple. She was rocking in his lap, her hands cupping the sides of his jaw. His arms were tight around her back, holding her as their kiss grew more intense.

"This is dangerous, naughty girl."

"Why?" Her voice was low and sultry. "We've still got our clothes on and you can't see anything."

"I'm not worried about me."

Her grip fell away from his face and her back straightened. "You think I can't resist you after just some kissing?"

Below Logan's black blindfold, his lips peeled back in a smile. "You did mention it was your gateway drug."

"Give me some credit. I bet I can handle it better than

ONE *more* RULE

you can."

His laugh said exactly how foolish he thought she was being. "Doubtful."

Oh, this was about to get interesting. Evie was focused and driven. She hated to lose, and she'd told me Logan was the same. I could sense the challenge coming.

She sat perfectly still as his lips skimmed over her neck, trailing kisses. "You seem awfully sure of yourself, Logan."

"If I wanted you to break your rule, we know I could get you to do it."

She pulled even further back from him. "Oh, do we? By all means, boss, go ahead and try."

Logan took a deep breath. "You sure?"

"I'm sure you're overly confident, yeah."

"All right, Evie." Logan smiled. "Challenge accepted."

Chapter FOUR

Saul parked the limo in front of a liquor store, and we left our blindfolded friends in the back while Dominic and I hurried in to pick up drinks.

"Champagne, whiskey, and rum," Dominic said to the clerk when we entered the tiny shop. He whipped out his wallet a second later and retrieved his credit card.

"What's the rush?" I asked.

"Gotta hurry before Evie caves and they're fucking in the back of the limo."

I latched a hand on Dominic's forearm, stilling him. "Evelyn. And what the hell makes you think that'll happen?"

The card was swiped, a receipt signed, and he hauled the paper bag of bottles into his arms. "Because I know Logan. He plays to win."

"Yeah, well, so does Evie."

The sapphire eyes sharpened on me. "Sorry, she doesn't stand a chance, but you want to make it interesting?"

My gaze narrowed to match his. "I'm listening."

"If Evie reverses her rule before, I dunno, say sunrise tomorrow..." Dominic's jaw ticked as he seemed to assemble the thought in his head. "You call your parents and try again to get a dinner or something between us worked out."

I groaned. Of course. "I don't know why you're making a big deal out of that. Seriously, you're not missing much with my folks. I have to force them to make time, you really want to spend two hours with people who don't want to be

ONE *more* RULE

there?"

His expression was fixed. "Do I want to meet my in-laws before the wedding? Yeah, Payton, I do."

"Fine. And if Logan breaks the rule and asks to have sex?"

He yanked open the shop door and held it for me. "Name your terms, devil woman."

What did I want that Dominic wouldn't give me freely? There was nothing. Sure, I'd like to skip the whole big wedding, but no way in hell was I going to deny him that. Then the thought formed in my mind. He'd been resistant to one request I'd made . . . "You and I have lunch with Joseph this week."

We strode toward the limo, and tension tightened Dominic's broad shoulders. Normally, I liked his possessiveness over me, but not where Joseph was concerned, because Joseph was my friend. A good friend. Yes, we'd fucked a bunch of times, but it had been empty sex for both of us, and stopped the moment Dominic walked into my life.

"Okay, you got it." Dominic tugged open the limo door. "But just know, you're gonna lose."

Really? I glared at him, but didn't bother to respond, and slid into the backseat. "What the fuck are you doing? Hands to yourselves!"

Evie and Logan scattered like teenagers caught in the act by parents, and Evie let out a nervous laugh. She probably thought I was kidding and giving her a hard time, but I was serious. The way Evie talked about kissing Logan made it sound like he could get her to do almost anything. Pre-Dominic, I thought she was crazy. Now I sort of understood.

Fuck, I did not want have to call my mom again.

Bass thumped repeatedly from beyond the black door that led into the club. We stood in the anteroom while Dominic paid our group's cover charge, and I pretended not to notice the bouncer's lewd stare.

Dominic's hand was abruptly on my ass, sliding over to rest on my opposite hip, and his scowl was directed at the bouncer. His possessiveness was showing in all its brilliant colors. I adjusted the paper bag in my arms, and the bottles clinked. "I can fuck you right here, if that will help."

Evie's mouth fell open. "Are you talking to me?" With the blindfold still on, she couldn't tell it was meant for Dominic.

"No, sorry." I laughed and helped her toward the entrance. She had one hand on my shoulder and the other laced with Logan's, but he was surprisingly quiet. Shit. "You know where we are, Logan?"

"The bottles gave it away."

Chicago had an ordinance banning alcohol from being served at the same establishment offering nude entertainment. All of the strip clubs in Cook County were BYOB.

"Keep your fucking mouth shut," I said. "Don't ruin the surprise for Evie."

The black door swung open and both the music and the roar of people got louder. I shuffled through, the future Mr.

ONE *more* RULE

and Mrs. Stone trailing right behind. Dominic and I scanned the large, open room, and he pointed across the way.

"There."

An open table waited near the stage. He hurried to claim it while I led the blind slowly through the crowded area, trying to keep Logan from tripping over chair legs. I ignored the looks of the other patrons who probably wondered what the hell we were doing.

"Can I take it off?" Logan said loudly over the music.

"I don't think this is the right crowd for that."

Did he just growl at me? "The blindfold, Payton."

"Not yet." I put my hands on his shoulders and shoved him down into a chair, then helped Evie to hers.

Dominic twisted the cap off the whiskey. "Evie, you want champagne? Or rum and Coke?"

I reached for the unopened bottle. "It's Evelyn, and she'll take a rum and Diet Coke."

Dominic smirked. "You're so bossy."

"You love it." We happened to arrive at the perfect moment, right as the last performer was exiting, so we had a moment of quiet. "Okay, blindfolds off. Time to look at some real women."

The deejay's voice blared over the music, announcing a new dancer coming to the stage as Evie pulled off her mask. I'd been nice enough to let her leave her crown in the back of the limo. Her eyes went totally white, they were that wide open. She gazed at the dim room, draped in garish red velvet curtains and mirrors, and the large stage with gold poles. Around us, the other club goers were curious.

Evie and I were the only dressed women in the packed audience.

The room felt smoky, although smoking wasn't allowed and I didn't see a fog machine running. It was a haze of sex and seediness. I hadn't felt this kind of dirty on me since my blindfold club days, and I'd missed it, just a little.

"Holy shit, I'm in a strip club," Evie said.

Dominic flagged over one of the servers. "You haven't been before?"

She shook her head slowly, her gaze locked on the woman who sashayed over, a round tray tucked under one arm. The waitress's other hand rested on her hip, barely covered by black hot pants. The piercing in her navel winked under a strobe light. Her hot pink halter top was more like a bra than a shirt, and the padding beneath pushed her boobs together, giving her a great deal of cleavage.

Her tips were probably killer; she was hot. I wondered if I should snap a picture and send it to Joseph. He'd trolled strip clubs in the past when he was first getting started, but he'd never found a girl who was seriously interested in the job, was drug-free, and reliable. Most of his newer girls came from referrals now.

"Hi!" the waitress said with a wide smile, her hand touching Dominic's arm. "What can I get for you, hon?"

My annoyance flared, but I stayed quiet while he ordered the Diet Coke, plus some glasses and an ice bucket for the table. On stage, a lanky blonde in a black bra and fuchsia G-string was strutting in her stripper shoes. I admired the tattoos running along her rib cage. On the right girl and in the right setting, ink was hot.

"How does she dance in those?" Evie whispered to me.

The sole of the shoe was black, but the seven-inch heel and tall platform base were both a matching fuchsia, which

ONE *more* RULE

glowed under the black light. The straps over the top of her foot were clear acrylic.

I shrugged at Evie's question. "Practice."

They didn't seem to give the blonde any trouble. She swayed with the sexy song pouring from the speakers, her lower body undulating to the rhythm. Her hands caressed her curves, teasing the removal. Fingers dipped below the G-string band at her hips, pulling it away for a second, only to return it into position, saving it for the big finish later.

I adjusted in my chair, setting a hand on Dominic's thigh, and his fingers curled over mine, holding my hand in place. Did he do this simply because he wanted to hold my hand? Or was he worried I would migrate further north to his cock? God, he knew me so well.

The stripper reached to set a hand high on the pole, wrapped her legs around it, and up she went. When she'd climbed to the top, her legs went straight out, parallel to the floor, and one knee bent, crossing over on top of the other leg. Her hands let go and she tipped back until she was upside-down, the pole clamped tight between her thighs. As she swung, her blonde hair fluttered behind.

There were murmurs of approval from the audience watching, and it built into a roar when her hands disappeared behind her back, and the bra was flung to the back of the stage.

"Holy shit!" Evie gasped and Logan chuckled.

The acrobatic work was impressive, and obviously I wasn't the only one who thought so. Guys lined up to throw crumbled dollar bills on the stage while she worked the pole. Her graceful moves, toned body, and tight breasts were sexy as hell.

"You're going to tip the stripper?" Evie asked when Logan dug out his wallet.

"No, naughty girl. You are."

I heard her hard swallow over the thump of the music. On stage, the stripper descended the spinning pole and planted her shoes back on the ground. She turned, bent over, and shoved her ass at the crowd, shimmying. More roars and cheers when she teased removing the tiny scrap of underwear once again.

This time she did it, exposing her bare pussy for everyone to see. Dominic's grip on my hand tightened subtly, then relaxed. "Fuck, she's hot."

I grinned. Did he know how much I loved hearing him say that? He was confident enough to know this wouldn't bother me. He was a man, hardwired to be attracted to tits and ass, and it seemed fucking stupid for him to hide it. Let him look and enjoy. I was. And my tits and ass were nicer, not to mention Dominic owned every inch of me, which made my ass a million times better.

Evie snatched the five-dollar bill from Logan and stood swiftly. She charged toward the end of the line of men waiting to tip, her face determined.

"That was . . . unexpected." Logan's expression had an edge of concern. Maybe he'd expected her to be too shy.

Like blood in the water, the men noticed her presence as a herd, and a few jaws dropped open. They parted, all gesturing for her to go to the front of the line. "Hey, ladies first," one of them said.

Evie was probably bright red. I couldn't see with her back facing us, but one of the guys at the front leaned over and said something close to her ear. She turned to look up at him wide-eyed, and Logan bolted out of his chair.

"Wait," Dominic called. "It's cool."

Apparently all the man had said to Evie was to put the money on her lips, which she did. Yeah, Evie. I laughed as the fully nude blonde took one look at my friend with a five-dollar bill on her face, and sauntered her direction. I had to believe every pair of eyes in the building were watching as the stripper palmed her breasts, and leaned into Evie so she was nuzzled between them.

"Fuck," Logan swore in appreciation. "I think I have another five."

The blonde's breasts were pushed together, so when the stripper stepped back, the five-dollar bill was stuck in her cleavage. People hollered for her to do it again, and someone yelled for Evie to take her top off. That sobered Logan quickly.

"Save your money," Dominic said. "We've got a private room we can head to whenever you want."

Logan's attention turned to Dominic, stunned and yet grateful, and it was clear he understood. A private room meant lap dances away from an unwanted audience. Right now there were dances going on in the open booths lining the left wall. Anyone could watch the girls as they slid their bodies over the customers, which was sexy, and also safer for the dancers. But the strippers always had bras and panties on. We'd get to see more in the private room.

Sure enough, Evie's face was flamingly red when she turned on her heel and marched back toward our table, but she held her chin up. As she made her way through the tables of men, they stared up at her, lust in their eyes, and it was clear that wasn't lost on her. Oh, there was power in being a desired woman. I knew about that. At times, the power could be downright addictive.

"Did you enjoy yourself?" Logan asked, his lips teasing a smile.

"Did you, boss?" Her voice was casual. "She smelled like strawberries."

The server came by with our glasses, and Dominic doled them out to the table. We drank and watched a few more performers, but no one held a candle to that first blonde who'd mastered the pole.

The shower show was nice. The ebony stripper had fantastic tits, and they looked even better when they were glossed with soap and water. As we finished our drinks, a redhead wandered past, dragging her hand along my shoulders.

"Do you or any of your friends want a dance?"

"Maybe in a little bit," Dominic answered for me. She smiled and flitted away, and he turned quickly to me. "Unless you were into her? Did I just make a horrible mistake?"

"Please. You know I've got my eye on someone else."

We hadn't talked about me getting a lap dance, he just knew. His eyes lit with amusement. "The blonde?"

I nodded as my hand tried to travel a line up to his dick, but he squeezed my wrist. "Control yourself." His expression went strict and hard. "Or I'll do it for you."

Evil, evil man. Saying that in his dark voice turned the volume up on my lust until it was deafening. Yet, he had a good reason to stop me. I'd feel awful if I got us kicked out and Evie and Logan's night came to an abrupt end.

"What do you think?" Logan said to Dominic, nodding toward the glowing neon sign that announced the private

ONE *more* RULE

rooms.

"Let's do it." Dominic gathered up our supplies and the ice bucket holding the champagne.

"We're leaving?" Evie sucked in a breath, probably horrified at how disappointed that had come out sounding.

"No, Evie," Dominic said. "I'm gonna buy Logan a lap dance. You get to pick out the girl."

The future Mr. and Mrs. Stone exchanged a glance. Choose wisely, Evie. I needed him to beg for sex so we could both win our little competitions.

Logan's intense eyes stared down at her. "You should do the lap dance. You're the hottest girl in here."

Dominic cleared his throat, but Logan remained unfazed. Thankfully Evie didn't fall for it, and she scanned the room, evaluating the girls working the floor. Her focus settled on a leggy brunette with shoulder-length hair and a pretty face, and sexy librarian glasses that were probably just for show. Yet they made her look cute and studious, which would definitely appeal to anal-retentive Logan.

"Her," Evie said. Her smug voice matched her expression, saying she was confident in this decision.

We went to the bouncer waiting beside the doorway, and I pointed out who we wanted to come join us in our private party. He nodded, wrote it down on a clipboard, and told us we were in room three.

The narrow hallway was dimly lit and bare bones, and there were a total of three rooms judging by the numbers on the door. I opened ours and was pleasantly surprised. It had a large tufted couch in red and two black chairs opposite it, with a low table in the center for our drinks. In the corner, a lit platform surrounded a pole. The hallway had been kind of gross, but this was nice.

Dominic and I each took a chair as Logan sat on the couch. "Come here," he said to his fiancé. "Are you okay with this?"

She let out a short laugh. "Me? Yeah."

It did seem silly to ask, given what we'd done, but at the same time I appreciated how important Evie's level of comfort was to him. He always did his best not to fuck up with her again.

"Let's establish rules," Logan said.

Evie gave him a dubious look. "You want more rules?"

"Guidelines," he amended. "I'm allowed to touch you. Kiss you. Everything except for sex is fair game."

Evie bit down on her lip and shook her head. "Part of the rule is no nudity—"

"As long as I don't violate that."

She didn't get a chance to answer him, for a sharp knock came from the door, and it swung open a half-second later. The leggy brunette with glasses. She was even cuter up close. Good.

She gave a shy smile, undoubtedly part of her act. "I'm Tracy. Someone wanted a dance?"

Dominic pointed out Logan. "He's getting married next weekend."

Tracy made the appropriate small talk that was probably club required, congratulating Logan. Thankfully, I didn't have to do that when I'd been seeing clients at the blindfold club, because I fucking sucked at talking.

The garter around Tracy's thigh was holding a lot of twenties, and I wondered how much she made a night. Nowhere near as much as I did at the blindfold club I was

ONE *more* RULE

sure, but she also made hers legally. She fidgeted with her lacy red bra and matching panties, as if anxious to get them off. Her curves were nice. Big breasts, and a round ass that begged to be touched.

"You sure you're okay with this, sweetheart?" Tracy asked Evie. I'd stopped listening to the conversation for a moment, she must have figured out the bride was right beside the groom.

Evie gave a devious smile and nodded.

"Okay," she said to Logan. "Can you open your knees? I need some room."

When Logan leaned back against the couch and relaxed his legs, Tracy put one knee between them, sliding it up and down, right over the fly of his pants. Her hands twisted behind her back and undid the clasp of her bra, and she held the cups to her chest for a moment before dropping the fabric away.

Her tits were immediately in his face.

Evie's breathing picked up as she watched the topless woman grind on her soon-to-be husband, but she didn't look anxious. Nope, she was getting turned on. She crossed her legs and put her hands together in her lap, almost as if she wanted to touch Logan but didn't want to get in the stripper's way.

Tracy's hands fondled her breasts, massaging them as she slid up and down his face. The music from the main stage was pumped into the VIP room and wafted from a speaker in the corner. She moved in time with the song that was all about fucking, letting her body give us a perfect visual.

When she straddled Logan's lap and rode him, everyone else in the room froze. Were they as unprepared as I was for how hot the scene was? Logan's hands splayed on her thighs around him, just resting there. Tracy didn't seem to mind.

"Fuck, Evie, kiss me."

A startled smile broke on her face. "Yeah? Are you having a hard time?"

"He's getting there," Tracy said, flashing a wink. Then she rose up on her knees, undulating while her hands ran up and down his chest, caressing him through his dress shirt.

I flinched when Dominic's fingers skimmed my knee. I'd been so engrossed watching the show I hadn't noticed he'd pulled his chair closer to mine. I leaned in and breathed in his ear, my words barely a whisper.

"I want to fuck you so bad right now."

"I know." He gave me a triumphant smile.

This was Dominic when he was most in control, and he loved his power. There'd been so many nights when we'd played with Akira and Yuriko, and I'd been writhing under his command, desperate to hold it together and begging for him to fuck me. He'd spent the first few months following Akira's lead when to reward, but his confidence had grown to no longer need advice. Dominic knew exactly when to give me what I craved, and how long to deny it to maximize our pleasure. Or make me crazy. Sometimes they were the same.

Tracy's hand flowed down the line of buttons on the front of Logan's shirt, over his belt, and . . .

"Shit." Logan groaned it through clenched teeth.

I raised an eyebrow at Dominic. Was that sort of thing allowed? Dominic shrugged.

"You're barely looking at her," Evie said to him. "Don't you think she's hot?"

I cut the chuckle off before it slipped out. She was

taunting him, trying to win her bet, and I fucking loved it. Plus, she was right. It seemed as if Logan was struggling and avoiding the scene as much as possible.

He groaned, low and frustrated. His hand hooked around the nape of Evie's neck and dragged her across the couch so he could crush his lips to hers while the stripper raked her fingernails over his zipper. I drew a deep breath in, sipping the air that was heavy with desire.

Tracy stood while Logan continued to deliver a passionate kiss, his mouth moving over Evie's with reckless abandon. Tracy turned and sat in his lap, rubbing her ass against the bulge of Logan's cock. Her creamy tits jiggled with her movements, and I fought to keep still. I wanted to touch her, or for Dominic to touch me, or both. My skin was tight with lust and I needed relief.

Evie moaned when Logan's hand trailed down her neck, over her collarbone, and settled on her breast. It was then that Tracy leaned to put her back against Logan's chest, her head resting on his shoulder opposite Evie. The dancer continued to squirm, and her movements were obviously having an impact on him.

Her head turned toward him, and I caught a flash of Tracy's tongue as it dipped out to lick the side of Logan's neck. He jerked and his free hand wrapped around her hip.

"Look at him," I whispered to Dominic. "Living the fucking dream."

He smiled back like the devil.

Behind the gyrating body, Logan fought for breath, or maybe to maintain his control. To go more than a month without sex, to kissing Evie while a nearly naked stripper humped him . . .

"Someone's a lucky girl," Tracy said, glancing at Evie. "His dick is huge."

Evie's face colored a shade of pink, and that was her only response. But the blush quickly faded when Tracy stood and swayed to the music, her fingers creeping beneath the band of lace at her hips. She rocked her thumbs down painfully slow, one side then the other, as her underwear began its taunting descent.

There was a sharp inhale from Evie when the red panties were lowered to mid-thigh, just below the money-filled garter. Tracy bent forward and set her warm hands on my knees. Her ass wiggled, shoving her bare pussy right in Logan's face. All the while she smiled at me behind her glasses.

"You're pretty fucking hot," I said.

She tossed her hair over a shoulder, and for a split second I wondered if she was bashful, but she laughed softly. "Thanks, girl."

"You never answered me," Logan said, his voice hurried.

Evie's gaze seemed unable to leave Tracy's hypnotizing pussy. "About?"

"The guidelines, naughty girl. I need to know . . . what's allowed."

The dancer's ankles came together. She stood straight, arched her back, and the panties fell to a heap at her feet. Holy fuck, she looked good in nothing but her money, glasses, and high heels. Dominic and I didn't get to look at the long, nude curve of her body for more than a few seconds. She turned to face the couch and knelt between Logan's knees while her hands ran along his inseam, working her way up.

"Fucking shit." Logan combed his fingers through

his hair and tipped his head back on the couch. Evie was sucking on his neck. Tracy's hands unbuckled his belt. His pants were unsnapped and a zipper dropped. Oh my God.

It wasn't clear if Logan was trying to sit up and stop Tracy, or if he was moving to make it easier. By the time he was sitting upright, the fully naked woman dropped down into his lap, right over his erection covered by a thin layered of black cotton.

"Shit. Shit, wait a minute," he said. His hands were on her undulating hips in an attempt to stop her. His eyes were hooded with lust, but still focused on Evie. But this didn't seem to bother his fiancé.

"Does she feel good?" Evie's smile was diabolical, and pride burned warm in my veins. It was exciting to see this side of her, the one who was powerful. It had come out for a moment in Logan's darkened bedroom that night last September when she'd let me join them. She'd pushed Logan right to the edge. Her voice was as commanding now as it had been then. "Tell me how bad you want me."

"Goddamnit."

"Tell me," Evie goaded, "what you want to do to me."

Tracy slithered over his cock, her pussy grinding against him. Were his eyes going to roll back into his head? He looked a half-second away from tossing Tracy away, slamming Evie into the couch, pushing her panties aside, and taking her in one, quick thrust.

He seemed like he might give up with his next breath.

"I want you to ride my fingers." He was panting now. His face had an intense, raw expression. "I want you coming on my face. Now, fucking tell me . . . is that allowed?"

"You'll violate the nudity—"

"No, naughty girl." He gave her a frantic kiss, as if he only had a fingertip's grip on his control. "Payton has blindfolds."

Of course. Kind of cheating, but not. Clever, Logan.

Chapter FIVE

Evie's blue eyes blinked at his question, and it was so clear. She wanted to say yes desperately, but also feared what giving him that power would do. I feared it as well. Men were most persuasive when they were on their knees.

"Answer me." It was a whisper from Logan, but his demanding tone made it sound loud.

"Yes," Evie said breathlessly. "But if you peek, I win."

Logan's smile was a million miles wide. "That won't happen, but I get it."

Tracy picked up the pace, sliding faster on him and the muscles along Logan's jawline flexed. He looked like he was enduring punishment.

The pads of Dominic's fingers traced circles on my knee and threatened to venture up onto my inner thigh. My legs parted slightly to make room and encourage, but he didn't take the bait. He just sat there, tracing his infuriating and teasing circles while I ached for his touch.

The song faded out and was replaced by another, and the waves of Tracy's hips slowed to a stop. "You want another dance, sexy?"

"No, thank you." It was tight and relieved from Logan.

Oh, hell no. He'd survived the lap dance, but I sensed he was wound tighter than a spring. Maybe he just needed another push.

"She wants a dance," I said, gesturing to Evie. "My treat."

The noise of protest that escaped Logan sounded suspiciously nervous, as Tracy lifted onto her knees and began crawling into Evie's lap. Who went statue-still with shock.

"You can touch me," Tracy whispered, her voice warm like honey. "Forget about club rules, I don't mind." Her knees were planted on either side of Evie's lap, and her hands tousled her light brown hair. Then her palms flowed down her neck, over her bare breasts, tweaking her nipples to keep them hard. Or maybe she simply enjoyed the sensation.

Tracy finished wandering her own body, and traveled over to the front of Evie's dress. Her fingers dipped inside the neckline. Evie's mouth fell open but no sound came out.

The woman glanced at Logan. "Is she shy?"

I snorted. "Only with strangers."

"Oh, shit." Evie's shoulders shuddered when Tracy latched her lips on Evie's neck. Hands moved under the neckline of her dress.

Dominic gripped my knee and tugged, drawing my focus to him. His dark, seductive look made my breath hitch. Lust hung heavy in the air, choked my lungs, and I was snared in his gaze.

"Get the fuck over here. You're too far away," he said in his rough, deep voice.

Too far away for him to undoubtedly torture me, but I went to him anyway, eager. I scrambled to sit sideways in his lap. His hold tangled in my hair and yanked me down into his kiss while his other hand slid up my leg, diving beneath my skirt.

Fuck yes.

I could hear movement on the couch that sounded as

ONE *more* RULE

if Logan was doing up his pants. Did he have blue balls, aching to be inside his fiancé? Because I could fucking relate. Whatever the female equivalent of that was, I had it. I needed Dominic. Somehow the restraint Evie had placed on Logan had an effect on me. It was like how denial instantly intensifies a craving.

Dominic feathered the lightest touch over my panties, but it was a bolt of static electricity on my sensitized skin.

"Yes," I whispered. "More."

His lips hovered by the shell of my ear. "Where?" His fingers brushed again. "Here?"

"Yes," I hissed. I gripped his forearm and squeezed. I both hated and loved his teasing.

"But you didn't say please, Payton."

"Fuck." I squirmed to try to get his fingers against me. I was soaking through the lace, and now I wished he hadn't given me permission to wear the underwear. The barrier between us needed to go, but Dominic held me firm.

Logan's voice cut through the fog, spoken with pride. "Naughty girl."

Holy shit. Evie had a hand on Tracy's tits, and her big, blue eyes stared up at the naked woman writhing in her lap. There was a tiny, unexpected spark of jealousy at this, which was ridiculous. I was the last woman Evie had been with. She and Logan hadn't invited anyone else to play after me, or so she said. I loved my best friend, but not in that way, and I'd gone on to play with other women, so wasn't I a fucking hypocrite?

"Is this okay?" she whispered to Logan.

His hand pushed down his erection, adjusting in his seat. "Are you serious? It's so fucking hot." He leaned in and swallowed her moan as he kissed her.

Dominic pressed a finger right to my clit, and I jolted. "Eyes on me, devil woman."

"Yes, Sir." I'd meant it to sound sarcastic, but this man made me fall apart. His expression was full of power and control as he stroked me. His fingers toyed with the seam, mocking that he'd move the fabric to the side and really touch me.

Speaking of mocking . . .

"Did you need something?" Evie said. I didn't dare take my eyes off Dominic, but I could hear the confidence in her voice. "You look like you need something."

"I'm fine, Evie." It would have been more believable if Logan's voice hadn't sounded uneven. "But watching you suck on her tits has me so fucking hard."

"What? I haven't done that."

"You're about to."

Evie blew out a breath. It was quiet, and then Tracy's low moan rang out. I wanted to watch what was happening. I was turned away to face Dominic, but he could see it all, and since I was in his lap, I felt the subtle jerk of his cock against my thigh.

His gaze flicked up to meet mine, and an indecent smile crept over him. "Your friend's licking the stripper's tits."

Why was I surprised that she'd done it? Obviously she didn't have a problem with women, and Logan had basically told her to. The good girl loved following his commands. But I was thrilled, too. This had been strategic on Evie's part, I was sure. She'd do what she could to win.

"And what about your friend? Does he look ready to break a rule?"

ONE *more* RULE

Even without seeing him, I could feel Logan's gaze boring into me. "No, he doesn't," he answered for Dominic.

But since I had obeyed my fiancé, he rewarded me. My breath evaporated in a shiver when my panties were tugged to the side and a finger plunged inside. My fingernails dug into his forearm at the welcomed intrusion.

"Slow," the rough voice echoed in my ear, just a whisper. "Don't rush me, or I'll stop. You don't want that, do you?"

I shook my head and clamped my teeth together to choke back the plea for more, and faster, and harder. God, all of what he'd give me, if only I had patience. Pleasure grew in slow waves, building with Dominic's painstakingly slow pace, and the thumb that teased my clit.

A soft moan slipped from my lips. If he expected me to be quiet, he was going to have to tell me.

"Ready to start revising the rule?" Logan's tone was wicked. "If I put my hand up your skirt, am I going to find your pussy wet and ready for me?"

Evie gasped. "Oh my God."

"That's not an answer."

Dominic's mouth captured mine, and his tongue slid past my lips. It possessed and tasted, and I returned the kiss with the same intensity he fed me. My next moan was louder, and two fingers delved into my greedy body. The stretch was delicious, but wasn't enough. His skilled fingers were amazing, but I hungered for the real thing.

Time began to blur. It was burned up by the heat Dominic was injecting me with. Abruptly the fingers retreated and I whined, but Dominic shushed me. He fucking shushed me—

The wet fingers were shoved in my mouth, cutting me off. I sucked them clean, and it was then I realized why.

Tracy stood in front of us, her bra and panties back on, and an expectant look.

"It's eighty," she said softly.

Dominic pulled out his wallet and pushed the Yen aside, digging out the American money. He counted out five twenty-dollar bills and handed them over. "Thanks."

"Thank you." She winked, thrilled with the tip. "Can I get you guys anything?"

"Yeah. There was a blonde on the main stage when we got here—"

"The one with the amazing pole skills," I interrupted.

Tracy slipped the twenties into her garter. "Ashley. I'll see if she's available to party with you."

As soon as she was out the door, Dominic reached for his glass of whiskey, and he chuckled right before tipping the glass back. It was because Evie had hurled herself into Logan's lap and his hand disappeared under her skirt.

"You can tell me you don't want to fuck," Logan said, "but your body says otherwise."

Evie sighed and clung to him. "You know I want to. This is all your fault."

"How's that?"

"You're the one with all the rules and who loves anticipation."

His expression was skeptical. Clearly he didn't believe her.

"Green..." She kissed his lips. "Yellow." She rocked her hips on him. "Red." Her hand gripped his cock through his pants. "You've taught me all about the build-up, boss."

Logan looked smug. His dark eyes studied her as he continued to move his hand between her legs.

ONE *more* RULE

"You let me know . . ." she said in a tight voice, "when you think you're so persuasive that I'm going to cave."

His short laugh was full of confidence. "I'll let you know when I start, but here's a clue. I'll have a blindfold on."

Evie's expression shifted into one of fear. "Wait, I've changed my mind. You can't go down on me."

Logan hesitated. "What?"

"No oral. Well, I can still go down on you—"

Oh, he did not like hearing that. His expression hardened. "Bullshit. You already set the rules, you can't go back on them."

His arm flexed and moved, as if he'd thrust his finger deep inside her. Evie inhaled sharply and balled his shirt into her fists.

"Fuck," she cried, twisting with pleasure and pain.

"No changing the rules during the game, naughty girl. Understood?"

It was barely a word from her. "Yes." It was immediately followed by a moan and she melted into Logan's embrace.

The door swung open without a knock, and in strolled the blonde on her black and fuchsia shoes. She was even better looking up close, but there was a cold, ruthless look in her eyes that I was a little too familiar with. This had been me at the blindfold club. Disconnected. Doing the job while being numb.

Ashley didn't have the people skills Tracy did—she was all business. "It's fifty for a two song dance. Forty for one song if you want me on the pole."

"Fifty," Dominic said. "My fiancé wants a dance."

She gave a plain look. "Sorry, I don't do women."

I . . . couldn't even. She took the money from Evie's

lips earlier without a problem. I found the girl's rejection annoying, even though it wasn't personal. She had every right to refuse, but . . . "You don't like money?"

Ashley's face soured, and when she wasn't smiling, she had a full-on case of resting bitch face. "I do, but I'm not into girls."

Her condescending tone was sharp as a knife, slicing both Evie and I, but she didn't appear concerned about it. Her gaze flitted from Dominic to Logan, and her whole demeanor changed. Her face lit up and her voice warmed like honey. "Do either of you guys want a dance?"

This girl made her living dancing for men, and she was a seasoned pro. One who assumed either Logan or Dominic held the money, and she'd have more luck getting extra dances out of the guy with the wallet if he was the one receiving.

"No, they don't want a dance." I snatched my drink off the table and slammed it. "But thanks for stopping by."

Her eyes widened with surprise. Surely she was used to being the most powerful woman in the room, but then, she'd never been in one with me.

"I can get on the pole for thirty." Like she was sensing the sale slipping away.

I gestured to Dominic. "You know what? He'll take a lap dance after all . . . for thirty."

Her eyes went narrow, but she didn't walk. How confident was she in her skills in getting more dances out of him? Apparently confident enough. She nodded in reluctant acceptance and strutted toward us.

Alcohol buzzed in my system, but when I rose to stand on my sexy high heels, I tried not to show the effects. I

ONE *more* RULE

rounded the chair so I could set my hands on Dominic's shoulders and lean over. It wasn't my first choice, but I liked this. It was a position of power and a front row seat to the dance.

Ashley's gaze paused on mine, and she issued a silent threat to keep my distance. Whatever, bitch. I'd touch him if I wanted to. Dominic would throw her ass to the ground if I asked him to do it.

The song changed and Ashley began her dance. Her feet moved side to side on those sexy heels while her hands wandered over her body. It felt . . . forced and robotic. Not alluring and seductive like Tracy's had been. Dammit, why didn't I just ask her to stay? Every second Ashley looked less and less attractive to me.

Her bra came off quickly and was cast to the floor as she remained on her feet, swaying to the music. Her hands stacked her blonde hair up on top of her head, and then it fell, cascading down as she shook her head, her tits bouncing slightly.

She spun on her heels and flopped down, putting her ass in Dominic's lap so she could grind on him. Would he even find this sexy? I felt bad for agreeing to the dance without checking with him first. I needed to make this better. Hotter.

I bent down and settled my lips a breath away from Dominic's, teasing my kiss. I even lowered until our lips barely touched, but didn't give him the pressure and intensity I knew he desired. His hand shot up, grabbed a handful of hair on the back of my head and forced me down so our mouths could crash together, while the other woman rocked in his lap.

But the impact of our kiss made my drunk ass stumble

on my heels. Shit! My hand latched onto anything to stabilize and keep me from falling. I found something soft, and warm, and bare.

Ashley's shoulder.

I yanked my hand back and straightened, but she jolted up out of his lap and spun to face me, anger flaring in her eyes.

"That was my bad," Dominic said. Ashley snatched up her discarded bra, not bothering to put it back on. "She didn't mean to—"

But Ashley fled without a word, exited the room in a huff, and the door slammed shut.

I blinked at Evie and Logan who were frozen on the couch, staring back at me, and since I was drunk, I no longer cared about my filter. She'd run from the room just because I accidentally touched her shoulder? "God, what a lesbian."

Dominic chuckled.

"You know what?" I said. "I think Tracy's hotter anyway, I'm sure we can get—"

The door opened and a thick white guy with no neck stepped inside, a sneer on his face. "Party's over. Time to go."

Chapter SIX

My mouth dropped open. "Are you fucking serious?"

The bouncer surveyed the room and his gaze landed on Dominic. "Yeah, you can't touch the dancers. You all need to leave."

"He didn't touch her," I said. "I did, and it was completely on accident."

The enormous man shook his head and crossed his powerful arms over his chest. "Not what the girl said, but it doesn't matter."

"This is bullshit."

"Are we going to have a problem here?"

Dominic's hands were on my waist, locking me in place, as if he knew I was a heartbeat away from getting in the bouncer's face. I drew in a breath to even myself out and remain in control. It was done, and no amount of talking was going to salvage it. "Nope, no problem." I put my hand on top of Dominic's, urging him to release me. "Let's go. I'm fucking exhausted anyway. The jet lag is catching up."

It wasn't possible to feel worse than I did as we were escorted through the club toward the main door. There were round tables near the entrance that had poles in the center so the dancers could entertain smaller parties, up close and personal. Ashley, back in her bra, was up on the table, dancing for a group of men.

I felt a little better when several of the guys turned my direction and watched me. From the annoyed expression on her face, I could tell she knew. These men preferred to look at me, fully clothed, over her in a bra and skimpy underwear.

The night air was cool as we waited for Saul to pull the limo up.

"Guys," I said. "I'm sorry."

Evie shivered in the breeze, but laughed. "It wasn't your fault. And think about how awesome the story is. I got kicked out of a strip club during my bachelorette party."

Logan's hands rubbed up and down her arms, trying to warm her. "Payton, it's not a problem."

"Of course not. You're just dying to get your blindfold back on."

Logan's grin developed slowly, and it looked seductive and sinister in the moonlight, much like a predator's, and Evie was his prey. "You're not wrong."

The limo pulled up and Saul hopped out, opening the back door. Evie and Logan climbed inside, but I motioned for Dominic to go next, and set a hand on our driver's arm.

"Can you just drive around for the next forty-five minutes or so? Stay in the city, but keep us moving?"

If it was an odd request, Saul didn't show it. "Sure, not a problem."

"Thanks." As I climbed in and shut the door, I wondered how much of our party he could hear behind the black privacy glass. Maybe he'd go home tonight and tell his wife about chauffeuring us from drag queen club to titty bar, or perhaps this wasn't that wild of a night for him. He was a limo driver in Chicago and might have driven all sorts of crazy celebrities.

"No more liquor for you." I tugged the champagne glass from Evie's hand. I didn't want it to be any easier on Logan.

In fact, I wanted him to need a crowbar to get her knees apart.

"What's going on?" The corners of her mouth turned downward. "Earlier you acted like you thought I was insane, and now you're on board?"

"Yeah," Dominic said before I could get anything out. "Now that she's got something riding on it."

Logan held an amused smile. "You made a bet?" His gaze settled on mine. "You're going to lose."

Dominic laughed. "I told her that."

Cocky pieces of shit, both of them. "Hey, fuck you. You both think you're so irresistible, why don't you try to seduce each other?" I sipped the drink I'd stolen from Evie as the limo took a turn and forced me to lean into Dominic. I set my hand on his chest and pushed off, righting myself. "Evie and I could watch."

It was like I'd insulted their mothers. Both men gave me an annoyed look, illustrating exactly how not funny that idea was to them.

"You're a bunch of hypocrites," I continued. "You love girl-on-girl, but you don't give us any guy-on-guy action."

Evie giggled at the thought. Shit. She sounded like I felt. Buzzing.

"Keep dreaming, devil woman."

I made a pouty face, but then I got an idea. The drink sloshed as I abandoned it in a cup holder and set my sights on Evie. She was sitting on the side bench, closest to the front of the limo, which meant I'd have to climb over Logan to get to her.

Strong arms ensnared me as I tried to move, and his low voice rumbled in my ear. "And where do you think you're going?"

"To get some girl-on-girl action," I whispered back, "since I didn't get any at the club." Instantly Dominic's hold was gone.

Logan eyed me with suspicion as I fumbled through the aisle. The car hit a bump and I tumbled into his lap.

"Don't mind me," I said, full of sarcasm. Which of course, he didn't. Logan made zero effort to help me, but perhaps he wanted to keep his distance. Dominic and I hadn't talked much about the fact I'd fucked his best friend, because it had happened months before I'd met the man who became my fiancé. But tension lurked in the quiet moments, and Logan didn't seem to know how to deal. It needed to not be so quiet.

"Get out your phone and put on some music," I ordered Logan. "Something sexy."

He didn't move. "What exactly is your plan?"

I flopped down on the seat between the bride and groom, edging Evie out of the way. "Evie's going to give me a lap dance."

Her laugh was bright and bubbly. She thought I was kidding? Because I wasn't.

The dark back seat glowed with soft light when Logan began tapping on his screen, and then a slow, seductive beat began.

"Come on," I said to her, my voice going husky. "Let's see if we can get Logan to come in his pants." How would Evie beg him for sex if he were already spent?

Logan's tone was dark. "You're hilarious. That won't happen, so there's no need to try."

"Logan," Dominic barked. "Shut the fuck up."

I grinned. Dominic hadn't gotten to see Evie and me together, after all. It was only fair.

"Okay." She flashed a smile as she shook her head. "Get ready for the least sexy lap dance ever."

I'd cut her some slack. She was a little drunk. Even though the limo was spacious, it was still the interior of a car and didn't leave much room. Plus, it was in motion and she had an audience.

But when she sat down on my lap and stared at me, like that was all she had, I laughed. "Yeah, don't quit your day job."

"Yes, please don't," Logan quipped.

Evie leaned over and put a hand on his leg to stabilize herself. "I wouldn't dream of it, boss."

I hadn't lied at the club; I was exhausted. So I needed to get the show going if I had any hope of getting Logan turned on enough to ask her to break her rule. My palm slid up her spine, and I buried my fingers in her soft, thick hair, only to clench a fistful and tug her head back. A startled noise erupted from her when I planted my lips on the side of her throat, right where her pulse pounded.

Both men straightened, and the mood in the back seat snapped from playful to serious in an instant. My other hand cupped the side of her face, holding her still as I sucked on her neck, and her heartbeat raced.

"Oh." It escaped from Evie on the lightest of sighs.

She smelled like citrus. The tip of my nose traced her delicate skin, and I exhaled. It drew a shiver from her, and power rose in my belly. I'd learned how much I liked being in control the first night Akira let me have it over his submissive Yuriko. Dominic wouldn't have an issue now, but how much control would Logan let me take?

Without releasing my hold, I softened my grip on the hair at the nape of her neck, giving her just enough leash so she could see both men gazing at us. Their lustful expressions only fed my power.

"Can I touch her?" I asked Logan, knowing his response would dictate what kind of response I got from her. If he were into it, she'd allow it. My hand not in her hair crept down to rest on her collarbone, and my fingers edged just inside the shoulder of her dress. Hinting exactly where I wanted to go.

"If it's okay with Evie."

It was a dangerous game I hadn't intended to play again, but I couldn't stop myself. The pads of my fingers glided over her smooth skin, traveling down the fabric of her dress until the round globe of her breast was in my hand.

She didn't stop me, thank God. Over the song playing on Logan's phone, I heard both men's breathing pick up.

"Shit," she mumbled. "What are we doing?" Only she arched her sexually starved body into my touch.

"Just having some fun." I squeezed and her nipple harden beneath her bra. So responsive. My mouth went back to her throat, and as I moved up, she turned her head down . . .

Our lips met. She kissed me.

Her warm, soft mouth tasted like champagne and sin, and her hands cupped my face. Passionate. Delicate fingers brushed my cheek, and abruptly she shifted in my lap. Moving so she could straddle my legs, and devote all of her attention to me. Did she have the same thought as I did?

Either way, it was thrilling. Once again her skirt was

almost to her hips, giving a hint of the dark panties she wore beneath. The new position made it easier to touch her tits, which I did. Her full C-cup breasts were so different from Yuriko's.

Evie rocked in my lap, stirring her hips, and grinding against me to the beat of the music.

"So you do know how to give a lap dance." Both of my hands massaged her breasts, pushing them together. "I think you should take off your dress."

Her eyes grew big.

"Nice try," Logan said. "You've had your fun, Payton." A surprised noise choked in Evie's throat when Logan grabbed her around the waist and hauled her into his lap, his eyes glinting with determination. "Dominic, do you mind if we sit there?"

He didn't. As soon as Logan was gone, carrying Evie to the seat in the rear, Dominic took his seat beside me. The song faded out and another replaced it. This one was still sexy, but sounded dirtier. Perfect.

"I need the blindfolds." It was an order from Logan.

Wait, no. Shit, I was going to lose. Evie settled into the seat and pressed back into it, her hands spread on her thighs. Then she crossed her legs and looked just as nervous as I felt.

"I left them in the club," I lied.

He'd seen me put them away, but even if he hadn't, it wouldn't have mattered. Logan was like me and could read lies easily. "No, you didn't."

I gave Dominic a traitorous glare as he reached into my purse, produced the blindfolds, and passed them to his friend.

"Why don't you," Logan said to Dominic, "check the view out the window. See what's changed in the city since you've been gone."

"The windows are tinted and it's night out."

"Then stare at the fucking ceiling. Don't look back here."

I laughed. Logan was just as possessive as Dominic, maybe more. My guess was Logan was about to remove Evie's panties and he didn't want Dominic to see anything.

"Okay." Dominic exchanged a smirk with me. "I'll try."

When Logan moved in to kiss her, she looked wary. She took the blindfold, but didn't put it on. "I don't have to wear it. Seeing myself naked doesn't violate the rule."

Logan's expression was ruthless, and his tone was that of a dominant. "Put it on."

Fuck. It made me hot and my hand curled on Dominic's leg. Logan slid off the seat so he was kneeling on the floorboard, his back facing Dominic and me, and obscuring Evie from view just as she donned the black mask.

"No cheating," she said, her voice wavering.

Logan slipped the thin strap on the back of his head and positioned his blindfold down over his eyes. "I've got mine on now."

I hopped up into Dominic's lap, which allowed me to see over Logan's shoulder, and to put Dominic's hand on my thigh, high beneath my skirt. His warm palm smoothed up and down, but didn't move inward. No, not yet. He'd stoke the fire until I was desperate, and then he'd make me burn.

Evie flinched when Logan put his hands on her knees and urged her to uncross them. Her lips pressed together when his hands moved upward, carrying her skirt with it, all the way until her black panties were exposed. I barely got a look before Logan wrapped his fingers around the sides and began tugging them off.

"No sex," she said. Who exactly was she telling? It sounded more for herself than for him.

"No sex with my cock," he clarified.

I held my breath as the panties were worked past her knees, and she pulled one leg out, leaving the underwear on an ankle. A tiny landing strip of hair covered her slit, and it was sexy as hell. At her sides, Evie's hands were clenched into fists. Her chest heaved rapidly.

"How's that view, Dominic?" Logan asked.

"Still tinted and nighttime."

"Great." Logan's palms trailed up Evie's legs, gently pressing her knees apart. When he reached the juncture of her thighs, his hands curled, and he raked his fingernails down the insides of her legs, sensitizing her.

She jerked. "Oh my God."

Logan bent, lowering his mouth to her knee, and his lips glided along the faint pink track marks he'd left on her pale skin. Goosebumps lifted on her legs, and she shuddered as he closed in.

"I've been dying to lick this pussy for the last thirty-seven days, Evie."

Her tremble increased with anticipation as he hovered so close she could surely feel his breath. Her hands moved to clench the sides of her dress, and she went white-knuckled.

A short gasp punctuated the backseat when his mouth latched onto her clit. And since Logan was nestled between her parted legs, and they both had blindfolds on, there was no one to know Dominic was peeking except for me. I grinned and shook my head, but he just shrugged. Sort of like, "Can you blame me?" I couldn't. It was so fucking hot.

"Oh, shit," Evie said. Her back bowed from the leather seats, which forced Logan to clamp his hands on her legs, keeping her spread. Her head tilted back and she panted for breath as his tongue worked its way through her valley.

He didn't stop or slow when her hand crushed into his hair. Either trying to drive him back or hold him in place, I couldn't tell. Her moans grew louder as his face nuzzled. He attacked her like a man desperate for her orgasm, which he probably was. Maybe he'd edge her for a while and make her insane with need, just as Dominic loved to do to me. The tough skin of his palm caressed my thigh, each stroke inching closer to my pussy.

"God, don't stop." Evie's whisper was more of a plea.

My legs opened and I shoved Dominic's hand where I needed it, pressing his fingers to my aching clit. I shifted in his lap, rubbing myself against him. But it wasn't enough.

"You're not allowed to wear panties for the rest of the night." His dark voice was low and in my ear, too quiet for our friends to hear. Yes. I scrambled out of the underwear and shoved the wadded fabric in my purse, then pulled his hand right back to where it had been. It felt so fucking good when he touched me, just grazing my clit. My nerve endings sizzled and begged for more pressure.

Evie's legs were shaking. Her knees had gone lax and spread wide, her whole body under Logan's command. Only one hand was on her thigh. The other was beneath his mouth, working a finger inside her. It was slick with arousal, sliding in and out easily.

He paused. "You want another, naughty girl?"

She bit down on her bottom lip and nodded, but since

he couldn't see, he continued to wait for an answer.

"Yes . . ." she said. "Oh!" Logan's first two fingers eased inside.

"Goddamnit," Dominic whispered. "You're so wet. Maybe I should have left your panties on."

I shuddered when not one, but two fingers pushed inside me. Before I could moan loudly, his palm curled around my mouth.

"Quiet, Payton. Not a sound."

His warm lips feathered kisses on my neck, sending waves of delicious shivers through me. So I sat there and watched Evie ride Logan's fingers and tongue, while Dominic fucked me with two thick fingers, and struggled not to make a noise. I tried to contain the bliss that crashed into me and threatened to erupt. Dominic always found a way to put restraint on me, knowing how much I craved it. It made my release so much better.

My thumb rolled circles on his hard cock through his pants. How far would he allow me to go? Could I undo his belt and fuck him under my dress in front of our friends? They couldn't see, but they could certainly hear.

There was a cry of pleasure from Evie, and a soft pop as Logan pulled off suction from her pussy.

"Tell me you want my cock," he said as he straightened. His hands undid his pants. "Tell me how badly you need it."

Her face was half-covered with the blindfold, but it twisted with agony. "Oh, God, Logan . . ."

Dominic and I froze when Logan's boxers were tugged out of his way and his large dick was gripped in a hand. A nervous cry tore from Evie as he ran the tip of his cock through her wetness, testing her.

"Wait," she blurted out. Her hands flailed, finding his shoulders.

He pumped his hips, sliding up and down through her folds. My pussy clenched at the visual. I loved how that sensation felt, the ridge of Dominic's cock when he teased, skin on heated skin.

And holy shit. Was Logan going to break the rule?

He was right there. Only a slight push of his hips and he'd be inside her. Evie gulped down air like she was drowning. Her desire and his need were thick in the enclosed space, blanketing us all.

"Don't you want to?" Logan's words were coated in persuasion. Evil man. She squirmed beneath him. "Are you trying to get me to fuck you, naughty girl?"

Her expression flashed with guilt. "Please."

"Please, what?"

"Do it," she begged. "Just for a second."

Dominic's warm breath was at the shell of my ear. "I told you." Dammit.

Logan continued his slow, mocking thrusts while not sliding into her. "What about the rule?"

"I don't care anymore. You win, Logan. Fuck me, please."

"Shit, Evie. I really fucking want to . . ." His hands clenched on her waist, tightening to hold her still. "But I won't."

She gasped. "What? Why?"

"Because I love you. I'm not going to risk any regret about tonight. What if we do this and you end up wishing we'd waited a few more days?" He reached a hand out, finding her face and guided himself to plant a kiss on her lips. "I promise I'll make it worth the wait."

Warmth spread through my chest, spiraling outward from my heart. Yeah, Logan was lucky to have Evie, but she was plenty lucky to have him, too. He always put her first, which to me was the definition of love.

I glanced at Dominic, who wore the same smile I probably had on my face. He'd give me whatever I needed, just as I'd do for him, no matter what.

"So," Logan said, "no sex until you make an honest man out of me. But I won't say no if you want to blow me right now."

She laughed and fused her lips to his. Their kiss was raw and powerful, and when she pulled back, she was grinning. But I knew her well. Beneath that blindfold, she was blinking back emotional tears. Her love for him was overwhelming.

"Where are you—" she said, but her words cut off as he bent back down. His tongue swirled where his cock had just been, and she twitched, like the pleasure had been intense. "Oh, shit."

He sank his fingers inside her, pumping them in a furious tempo, and his mouth rotated on her clit, hinting how much work was going beneath his lips. She bucked on the seat, groaning.

Her moans swelled with each passing second. "God, I'm close," she said. "I'm so fucking close."

It only made Logan increase his efforts. His hand not inside her body wandered up her stomach, grabbing a handful of her breast. That seemed to be the final straw to tip her over the edge.

"Fuck!" She seized as tremors tumbled down her legs. The muscles along her calves strained with the orgasm until she collapsed back against the seat with an enormous sigh. Her mouth was slack, and she panted for air.

Watching the ecstasy rip through her flipped a switch on Dominic. His fingers pulsed inside me, and teeth sank into the flesh of my earlobe, so his breath filled my ear. My mind couldn't focus on anything but this man. I groaned quietly into his rough palm that was covering my lips.

"Touch your pussy. Let's make this body come."

It was a command I was happy to follow. I buried my fingers in between my legs, rubbing the swollen nub, needing relief. God, his hands. The one fucking me was building my climax, but the one keeping me quiet was so dominating and hot.

Logan sat on the seat beside Evie, and she didn't waste any time switching positions with him. Her knees were on the floor, the panties still wrapped around an ankle, and her hands gripped his hard cock in the moment before it disappeared into her mouth.

It came on a low voice from Logan. "Fuck."

Was there something wrong with me that I liked watching this? I enjoyed seeing her head bob on him, and loved listening to his heavy breathing. I was already unbearably turned on, but then Logan gathered her hair up into a makeshift ponytail, holding it with a strong hand while she sucked him. It was so hot, it made me sweat. He controlled her pace, and the leather seats protested when he thrust up into her mouth.

All the air in the interior of the limo seemed to have disappeared, and in this vacuum, electricity crackled with intensity as both Logan and I approached orgasm. I wasn't trying to time it with him, but I also wasn't in control.

ONE *more* RULE

Dominic was, absolutely.

"Who's going to come first?" His gravel whisper asked.

"I think it should be you."

Desire burned across my skin, glossing it, and I hungered for my release. Everything ached and focused in on the end goal. The tingling, lightweight sensation that happened just before orgasm fluttered in my belly.

"Mmm . . ." I moaned through Dominic's hand, and let the pleasure take me. I convulsed in his embrace, slowed my own touch, and pressed my fingers hard to my pulsing clit. My eyes pinched shut and everything felt warm and amazing as I exploded.

As it faded, I inhaled a breath slowly through my nose, and the hand fell away from my mouth.

"Yes, just like that," Logan said through clenched teeth. "I'm gonna come." His grip guided her to go faster, and faster, and . . . "Shit, shit!"

His moans built into a crescendo and peaked, and he held her firm as he came, her jaw locked around him. It prolonged the aftershocks of my orgasm, even as Dominic's fingers retreated. But when he withdrew, it took the last of the energy from my body. Exhaustion stormed in and made itself home.

What about Dominic?

I set a hand on the bulge of his pants, stroking down, but he took my hand in his and stopped me.

"Can I be honest?" he said. "I'm fucking tired. I need a raincheck, devil woman."

He couldn't be more perfect if he'd tried. "Thank God. I am, too. You just saved yourself from a lackluster blow job."

His eyebrow lifted. "Blow job's still a blow job." But

his arms tightened around my waist, holding me close. "Tomorrow. You better give me your A-game."

I shrugged and tossed my hair over a shoulder. "I don't know. I don't just give that to anybody."

The embrace was gone, only so he could flick my tattoo and deliver the tiny sting that reminded me how much I loved him. Even though he knew I didn't need it.

Chapter SEVEN

I stared at my phone, gnashed my teeth, and slowly lifted my gaze to meet Dominic's. "They're late."

"Give them a minute. You know how traffic can be."

We sat in the back of the crowded restaurant and nursed drinks while we waited for my parents to arrive. I'd made the call yesterday morning while Dominic hovered over me, ensuring that a decent effort was put in on my part. And I couldn't fault him for wanting this, but I hated it. My parents were going to disappoint us, and although I wasn't responsible, I still felt that way by association.

The waiter came by and asked if we wanted to order lunch, but Dominic shook his head and the waiter left.

"You think it'd be rude to order without them?" I asked. Dominic's expression was pointed, but I shrugged. "Well, I think it's fucking rude that they can't tell us they're running behind."

I was halfway through my second glass of wine when my phone rang. I glanced at the number and groaned. "One guess who it is." I swiped to answer the call and tried not to seethe. "Hey, where are you?"

"Payton," my mother said. "Your father's in a deposition that's taking a lot longer than he thought it would. Are you already at the restaurant?"

Was I—? Seriously? "Yeah. You said one o'clock."

She sighed. "I don't know when he's going to be finished, and he's got to be in court by three. This case has been such a mess, I told him he should have given it to one of the other partners."

"So you're not coming."

From across the table, Dominic's blue eyes studied me, gauging my response. All he wanted was to meet my parents. We'd flown ten thousand miles from Japan, and they couldn't make it twenty blocks from my father's law firm.

"We were looking forward to it," my mom said, "but it's been such a busy week. I'm sorry. I feel just awful about it."

"Yeah?" I was done with this bullshit. "You should feel awful." I pressed the End Call button and dropped my phone on the table. Surely my mother was on the other end wondering what had happened. I'd never talked to her like that before, but I'd also never felt more let down by them.

"I'm sorry," Dominic said.

His unnecessary apology only made me angrier. "You're sorry? For what? Wanting my parents not to be dicks?"

I said it too loud and the couple at the table next to us glanced over.

"No more wine for you." Dominic gave me a lopsided smile. "You know, it's easier to talk like that when no one around us speaks English."

"I told you this would happen."

He blinked, but his face remained unchanged. "You did." He flipped open his menu casually. "So, we tried, Payton. We'll see if they change their attitude when they want to see their grandkids."

Grandkids.

We both wanted children, and we'd talked about it in the future, but it continued to throw me off balance how settled and comfortable he was with the idea. Sometimes I'd catch myself staring with disbelief at the enormous ring on my finger. I was engaged, I had to remind myself. I'd found another person who willingly wanted to be a part of my life. Shocking.

His carefree demeanor, and the lunch we eventually ordered, diffused some of my anger. It was pointless to get worked up, and I tried to emulate Dominic's easy mood.

"So, I've been thinking," I said as we finished up our plates. "We both technically won the bet about Evie and Logan."

Dominic leaned back in his chair and crossed his arms. "How do you figure that?"

"The no-sex rule. It didn't get broken."

A lazy smile grew on his lips. "Fine, devil woman. I'll have lunch with Joseph, but only because you want us to. Let's be clear. You did not win that bet."

"Whatever." I climbed out of my chair, and was about to tell him I was heading for the restroom, when something caught my eye. Not something, but someone.

Holy shit.

He wove through the tables, moving quickly toward me, a blur in an expensive suit. "Payton."

"What the fuck?" I stared in disbelief.

He grinned, surprised. "Wow, nice language." His glance went from top to bottom. "And, wow. You look great."

Dominic's hand was warm on my waist, but his expression painted in a scowl at this man he didn't know. I would have laughed if I could get over what I was seeing.

"You must be the fiancé. I'm Kyle McCreary." My brother extended a hand.

Once the information settled in, the tension in Dominic's shoulders relaxed and a smile broke on his face. He took Kyle's hand and shook it. "Hey, yeah. Dominic Ward."

"Okay," I said. "What are you doing here?"

"Mom told me what happened. I thought I'd see if I could catch you before you left."

There was a thin gloss of sweat on Kyle's forehead as if he'd hurried, and the purple plaid tie he wore with his gray suit was askew.

"So you ran from New York all the way to this restaurant?"

Kyle's soft smile froze. "No, I live here now." He pushed his suitcoat back so he could rest his hands on his hips and catch his breath. "You didn't know?"

He looked so different from the last time I'd seen him, which had been . . . when? My college graduation? Kyle's hair was more like Dad's, the color of maple syrup. He'd let it go long on the top and it was a little wild. Soft curls turned up at the ends. I couldn't tell if he'd skipped shaving for the last three days, or if it was perfectly maintained scruff.

Either way, it was a good look on him.

My arms moved without thought, and suddenly I was hugging him. Kyle stood straight and immobile, confused. My family did not hug. But then again, I'd always been the black sheep.

"No, Mom didn't tell me," I said. "She's too busy, I guess." I stepped back from him and curled into Dominic's embrace. "When did you move?"

"About six weeks ago. Dad got me a position with his firm."

"What happened to New York?"

ONE *more* RULE

Kyle's eyes clouded with an emotion I couldn't interpret. He looked . . . unhappy? But in a flash, the emotion was replaced with an empty one. "That's a story for later." His gaze held mine. "Look, I can't stay. My schedule's crazy while they're bringing me up to speed on my caseload, but . . . hell. We haven't seen each other in a while."

We certainly hadn't. My older brother and I weren't close growing up. I'd done my own thing while Kyle had been the golden boy. I didn't envy him; the crown seemed heavy. Mom and Dad laid enormous pressure on him, so I understood when he'd high-tailed it out of Chicago, not a week after graduating law school. My parents felt disrespected he hadn't come to the firm that carried the McCreary name.

But that had been years ago. Now he was back?

"So you ran twenty blocks in a suit to see me?" I asked.

"Mom said you were upset." He took a deep breath and smoothed a hand down his tie. "Mom and Dad don't get it. They think their stuff is more important than anyone else's. I used to try really hard to make them understand, and honestly, my life got so much easier once I stopped."

My mouth dropped open. It was the most honest I'd ever heard him, and he made his living spinning truths and twisting words.

"I also came to meet Dominic." Kyle's focus shifted to my fiancé. "As her brother, I'm supposed to threaten you with bodily harm if you don't treat her right, but that's not really my style. So enjoy my threat of litigation instead. I'm very good, and it wouldn't be pleasant."

"Aw, you're sweet," I said, my voice mocking. "But Dominic's smart. He knows if he fucks up with me, I'd be his biggest threat."

"Yes," Dominic said instantly.

Kyle blinked again at the profanity. Not like he was offended, but more amused. Shit, how far apart had we'd been these last few years? He barely knew me anymore, and I'd never really known him.

"Okay, well, that's good, I guess." Kyle fiddled with his watch and checked the time. "I have to run. As in, literally."

"Thank you for coming," I said, hoping my voice matched how sincere I felt, because I was a little blown away.

"Should we grab drinks some night this week?" Dominic asked, but Kyle shook his head.

"I'd like that, but everything's a mess with the move. You two will be back for good in a few months though, right? We could do it then."

"Sure."

We said our goodbyes, and I watched Kyle go. It was such a simple gesture for him to come over, and yet it meant so much.

Dominic had a strange half-smile on his face.

"What is it?" I asked.

"Running here and back just to say hello. Your parents don't get it, but your brother does."

"Yeah," I said. Who would have thought?

The premium leather of my driver's seat was buttery soft. I'd narrowly avoided reunion tears when I'd picked my

ONE *more* RULE

car up from Logan's place. Well, technically, our place. Evie and Logan would move out in mid-December so Dominic and I could move in when we returned from Japan.

I felt bad about kicking them out, but only for thirty seconds. The view was to die for, and Logan had known this day was coming since leasing the place from his friend.

"It looks different in the daylight," Dominic said, gesturing to the blindfold club entrance. He wasn't wrong. The black door looked smaller, and the wear on the façade seemed greater in the harsh light.

"Yeah, this place is way less sexy during the day." A fact I'd discovered the first time Joseph had asked me to fill in for him. I hadn't a clue why Joseph wanted to meet here now, but since the club was a good twenty-minute drive from our hotel, and I had my hands on my Jaguar F-Type, it was fine with me.

"Any chance you'd let me drive the car back to the hotel when we leave?" Dominic's hopeful expression wasn't enough to pry my grip from the steering wheel.

He hadn't driven a car in almost two years. "No way, get your own."

"Half of this car will be mine when we're married."

I shut off the engine and let my expression go serious. "Yeah, the passenger half."

We hurried across the street and through the front door that Joseph left unlocked for us. It was dark except for the security as we strolled through the bar and down the hallway of doors. The silence and poor lighting further detracted from the sex appeal.

To the left were the holding lounges, and to the right were the client rooms. I'd met Dominic in Room One. A smile warmed on my lips as we passed the door decorated with the brass six, the room where Dominic asked me to be his wife.

"Joseph?" I called, leading Dominic upstairs.

"In here."

Not in his office, but across the hall in the large dressing room. He stood by the bar lining the far wall, his back turned to us. His suit jacket was cast aside on a chair, and as he poured himself a glass of whiskey, I could see his sleeves had been rolled back. This was as close to casual as Joseph got.

"Hey."

My voice forced him to turn. He probably appeared composed and maintained to Dominic, but like the last time I'd seen Joseph, there were faint edges around his eyes. He looked... weary. Not that I'd say that to him. Joseph was all about power, and he'd view it as weakness.

He smiled. "You got him to agree to come."

"Of course," I said. "My boy-toy does whatever I tell him to."

The snap on my hip was sharp and biting. Dull pain lingered on my tattoo, so I glared up at the blue eyes watching me. "Okay, ow."

Dominic looked smug. "Watch it."

"You watch it," I echoed back like a four-year-old.

Joseph carried his drink in one hand and strode toward us, pretending he hadn't just witnessed the immature exchange. "Dominic," he said. "I'm Joseph Monsato."

"I remember." My fiancé's words were tight. "Everything about that night was pretty hard to forget. You know, except for those ten minutes after the bouncer's right hook."

They'd met face to face in the front lounge when Dominic first arrived at the club almost a year ago. It was protocol with walk-ins, plus Joseph liked to evaluate potential clients to match them with the right girl. That meeting had been fine, according to Dominic, but the way he'd left the club was still a sore subject. He'd spent the whole night trying to find me, his head throbbing with a black eye, all because of Joseph.

"I'm sorry about what happened," Joseph said, his expression genuine. "I didn't handle it well when Payton said she wanted to leave. Your fiancée was a big part of this place, and also my friend, and . . . I wasn't sure how the fuck I was going to get on without her."

Joseph didn't mean it sexually, of that I was sure. Yet his admission made my breath stall in my lungs. When I'd left the club, I hadn't just quit, I'd effectively abandoned Joseph. I was at a loss for words, which had to be a fucking first.

"It was good, though," Joseph continued. "For me, and most definitely for her."

Dominic shifted his stance. He didn't seem to be faring much better than I was with the seesaw emotions between resentment and surprise. "Uh, yeah."

Joseph's attention sought mine. "I bet you want to know why I asked you here."

"The question had crossed my mind."

"I need a favor, and unfortunately, I need it from both of you."

Well, he was just full of surprises today. "What is it?"

The amber liquid sloshed in Joseph's drink as he swirled his glass. "I hired a new girl, and I can't get a read on her." He paused to take a sip. "Usually I can tell whether or not they'd be good, but this one . . ."

"How'd she do with her . . ." I wasn't about to remind Dominic how the girls at the club got their spots. Several months ago I'd had too much vodka, or 'truth serum' as he called it, and spilled all the gritty details about the club. "With her audition?"

"Christ," Dominic growled.

But Joseph's face was stoic. "She didn't audition. Regan's only interested in being a sales assistant. She's made it clear she won't get on the table."

As far as I knew, that was a first. All girls started on the table. "Why not?"

"She says she has a boyfriend, but I don't think that's her reason."

"Okay, what is?"

"She's not submissive," Joseph said.

I could sense Dominic's impatience with all of this, and tried to get right to it. "So, what's the favor?"

"I'm hoping you'll get on the table," he said, his dark gaze trapping mine. "And let Regan negotiate the deal when Dominic tries to buy you."

Chapter EIGHT

Regan was a redhead, her hair fire engine red with streaks of copper. She had gorgeous, big blue eyes and high cheekbones, and a slender frame. But beneath her simple black suit dress, I could see power lurked. This woman had a strict workout regimen.

Her sleek nose and bow lips made her look regal. She was beautiful, which was good. Her looks would help her during negotiations. A little older than me, but still young.

"You've done this before?" I asked her as I stripped off my clothes and hung them in the empty, open-faced locker in the dressing room. Dominic had been sequestered into one of the holding rooms downstairs, while Joseph went to his office.

My fiancé hadn't been thrilled with this plan, but I felt like I owed Joseph. I'd abandoned him twice in the last year, first when I'd quit, and once again when I'd gone back to Japan. So I told Dominic I wanted this, and gave him the reminder that he'd be running the show when I was on the table. Total control over me.

So, he was on board.

Regan's voice was pleasant. "I shadowed with Nina and Tara several times. I know I'm new, but trust me. I'll get the most I can out of him."

Even though it came off sounding arrogant, I liked it. Sales were all about confidence, and this woman had it in spades.

I slipped an arm into the silk robe while her gaze lingered at the tattoo on my hip, but she said nothing. She seemed comfortable when I'd gotten naked, not staring, but not averting her eyes either. Like she was assessing me as a product, which was good. I dug through my black hole of a purse until I located a tube of lipstick and went to the mirror to apply it.

"You're sure you're up for this?" she asked. "Joseph said you haven't been back very long."

I pressed my lips together, spreading the color evenly. We'd decided for a cover story that I'd left Dominic back in Japan, returned to Chicago bitter from the breakup, and flat broke. I was ready to get back to the blindfold club and start earning money.

"Fuck yeah. I might be a little rusty, but I haven't forgotten what to do." I gave her a wink. Not that there was all that much to it. I'd be bound, blindfolded, and not supposed to speak.

"All right. Let's go make some money." She hooked in her earpiece and motioned toward the door.

If Regan was nervous about her first solo sale, she didn't show it. Her heels clicked steadily over the floor when she pushed open the door to Room Two and led me inside. She moved with practiced efficiency to prepare. First, the lights, then the thermostat, and finally she went to the cushioned table in the center.

A drawer squeaked as I slipped the robe off and hung it on the hook. Regan already had the straps tethered to the anchors on the table when I made my way toward her.

"Joseph mentioned the client is already in the holding room," she said, subtly telling me not to dawdle. Wealthy men didn't wait for pussy. "Did he tell you anything about the appointment? I figure he's someone important for Joseph to schedule in the middle of the week."

"Maybe," I said with forced casualness. It was hilarious how excited I was about the favor. Dominic and I were both going to enjoy this role-play.

Regan rushed through the final stages of setup so I was bound and had the blindfold in place, and she signaled Joseph through her comm that we were ready. There was no sound from her other than her soft breathing. She didn't bother to move to the chair in the corner to wait, knowing it wouldn't be long.

In the dark and quiet, my body began to respond. Goosebumps pebbled on my skin and anticipation hardened my nipples into knots. I licked my lips, waiting impatiently for him.

"Good afternoon, sir," Regan's voice purred.

I hadn't heard the door open, but it shut behind him and Dominic shuffled a few steps closer. My legs slid together, rubbing my knees against each other as desire corded around me. Would he leave the blindfold on this time? The straps, I was sure. I'd called the shots both times we'd been here before, and he wasn't going to give me an opportunity to do it a third time.

"Do you like what you see?" Regan asked sincerely. Not pushing, not yet.

"Yeah, she's pretty cute."

My face scrunched under the blindfold. What the fuck was that, cute? I held my tongue, but I'd let him hear about it later. He was probably grinning at how hilarious he thought he was. That was, if he wasn't blushing.

"Pretty cute?" Regan's words were dubious. "I think she's gorgeous."

"Yeah, all right, she's really fucking hot." Better, Dominic.

"You two would make quite the pair. It looks like you're in fantastic shape, if you don't mind me saying. Do you work out, play sports?"

Good. Regan used the code to communicate that he was attractive when she dropped the sports mention.

"No sports. I'm more into lifting. So, how does this work?"

She paused. "You haven't been to the club before?"

"No." Dominic took a step closer. "I almost didn't come in. This place didn't look like I expected it to."

It wasn't all that much of a lie, and I appreciated the detail. He was doing a decent job of selling it.

"Well, I'm glad you did. Is that beautiful Jaguar out front yours?"

"Sure is."

I could hear the fucking smile in his voice, and it was insanely difficult not to jolt against the restraints or call him out. Oh, he was going to get it when these straps were off.

"Nice," she said. "Fifty thousand."

He gave a sharp noise of surprise. "Are you asking if my car was fifty thousand dollars, or is that the price—"

"It's for her."

Holy shit, what the fuck was Regan doing?

"That's . . . too much." He stumbled over the words, as if he wasn't sure what was going on. Yeah, me too.

"You're saying you don't think she's worth that?"

A frustrated sigh slipped out. He'd told me long ago the

ONE *more* RULE

negotiations made him queasy. He didn't like assigning a dollar value to me. This was supposed to be fun. Pretend. Her question made it a little too real.

"I'm saying . . . I'd feel more comfortable paying five."

Her heels clicked as she glided closer to him. "I understand." Her warm hand rested lightly on my ankle. The indication that she thought he was willing to pay a lot more, which he had agreed to once.

Her hand squeezed, prompting me to respond. I shook my head.

"I'm sorry, she's not willing to accept the offer. Would you like to try again? How about sixty thousand?"

"What? That's more."

I couldn't understand what her game was, and broke the rule about staying quiet. I tried not to hiss it at her. "What are you doing?"

"Joseph told me to try to get as much out of the client as I could." Her direct voice was stunning. "I believe this man would pay every last cent he had for you." Oh my God. "Am I wrong?"

The question seemed to be for Dominic. He sighed. "Nope."

"You're her boyfriend?" she asked.

"Fiancé."

"Fuck," I said, squirming against the straps. "What tipped you off?"

"Lots of things. He didn't look at your tattoo, which is interesting, so that made me think he'd already seen it. There's no security on the premises, which says Joseph trusts this man with you." She paused. "Also, I could tell he lied about the car. Even if I couldn't, it was too much coincidence. I saw the Jaguar logo on your keyring as you were going through your purse upstairs."

A feminine hand was on my wrists, tugging at the Velcro.

"The biggest giveaway," she continued, "is the way he looks at you. Can't take his eyes off of you."

The command from Dominic was quiet, but firm. "Stop. I'll do that."

Yeah, he'd undo my restraints . . . when he was good and ready. I took in a deep breath. "Tell Joseph he should hire you."

She gave a half-laugh. "He just did." She must have meant through the comm in her ear. "Have fun, you two."

Heels tapped out on the hard floor, growing quieter with each step, and the door fell shut. I flinched when fingers skimmed across my belly and up between the valley of my breasts. He gripped my chin and set his soft lips against mine.

"I would, you know," Dominic said. "Pay every last cent I have for you, Payton."

"I told you, I don't want your money."

His hot mouth sucked and licked at the base of my throat as it journeyed downward. "Yeah? What do you want?"

"For starters, I want my ring back. And then I want your cock."

He chuckled and the mouth vanished. The cold ring was slipped back onto its home on my finger, and I clenched my hand tight around it. It'd been off for twenty minutes, but it felt like eons.

"Okay, now that cock."

His lips were back at my collarbone, inching over my

ONE *more* RULE

skin. "You," the stubble of his unshaven face rubbed against my breasts, "are not... fucking in charge."

"Shit!" I cried as he nipped at the underside of my breast, hard enough it might have left a crescent shaped mark. His physical mark on me to match the emotional one he'd left. Dominic stained my soul, and I loved it. Electricity spider-webbed from the sting, and my veins flooded with heat.

My hands curled around ribbons holding me down as his fingernails scored painlessly across my stomach in a straight line toward my pussy. His light touch was worse than his firm one. The ache choked my lungs and left my head swirling with need.

Inch by inch.

His mouth followed his fingers down and he inhaled deeply, like he was trying to memorize my scent. The pads of his fingers worked over the inside of my thighs, my hips, and dragged slowly from one spot to another just above my slit. Teasing. Tormenting.

"Touch me," I whispered.

He didn't. His palms smoothed down my legs and back up again. I urged my knees apart and the leather protested quietly. The throb in my clit was intense, fueled by his warm breath that I could feel pouring over me.

"Dominic," I whined.

Those fucking hands continued to explore and linger, never straying to where I was desperate for them. His lips skimmed the inside of my knee. Sparks danced across my nerves as two fingers brushed upward in a line along my thigh, starting a tremble in my legs.

"Please." I begged it on a shuddering breath.

"This is how I like you. Watching you trying to keep it together." There was another nip on my thigh, but this one was soft and seductive. "Let's play a little game, Payton. I'm going to undo one of your straps."

It was hard to think through the fog of lust. He was going to set me free? The use of one hand meant I could easily undo the other strap or pull off the blindfold. I'd only have the illusion of restraint.

"I'm going to make you come," he said. He kissed the spot where my leg joined my body. The muscles low in my stomach clenched in response, so hard it was almost painful. "If you touch me, or yourself, you don't get to come the rest of the day."

I swallowed a gulp of air and bit down on my bottom lip. I almost preferred that he keep me bound. I didn't trust myself. But the Velcro tugged open with a loud scratchy noise, and his hand closed on my wrist, pinning it to the mattress-top.

"It's simple. Your hand stays here. Can you obey?"

My chest was heaving and my heart raced. "Yes, Sir."

He issued a noise of approval. I didn't call him Sir often as if he were my Dom and mean it. I liked rationing the word so it carried more power and weight when used.

"Yes," I cried. My back arched up off the table and my head tipped back. His soft, sinful tongue licked and swirled. It fluttered on my clit. I probably looked like a woman possessed when he fucked me with his mouth, but it was true. I was completely possessed by him. Two thick fingers crept inside. The first inch. And another. Behind closed eyelids, colors spun with my pleasure.

But the warmth of his mouth retreated, causing me to

ONE *more* RULE

collapse back against the cushion-top.

"Oh . . . my . . . fuck."

He wasn't playing fair. A third finger nudged down, touching my asshole while his fingers were fucking my pussy. I swallowed hard, and commanded my hand to stay in place. I wanted to rub my clit as his finger began to intrude there, filling me full. My orgasms with anal were much more intense, but I wouldn't get there on penetration alone.

I began to writhe when he had two fingers in each entrance. His languid pace was diabolical, and I pictured him bent over the table between my legs, propped up on one arm as he fucked me with the other. His gorgeous eyes would be watching my every move. Every gasp of breath I took.

My head turned and I moaned it into the side of my arm. "Oh, God, please."

It was killing me not to set my fingers on my swollen clit. It would probably take me two circles of my frantic fingers and I'd come apart. He knew this. He was pushing me as he liked to do.

"You're so fucking hot, I can't stand it," he said in his rough, deep voice.

I cried out in relief as his other hand cupped my pussy, his thumb rolling circles on the nub that was the center of my pleasure.

"Scream for me," he commanded.

Holy shit, I did. It ripped from my throat and echoed in the soundproof room, so only he could hear how much ecstasy he'd drawn out of my body. I convulsed on his fingers as bliss tore me apart, and the sensation went on.

And on.

Oh my God.

I screamed again as the second wave of pleasure crashed into me, leaving my mind blank. All I could do was shudder and endure as my body took control. Flashes of white decorated my eyelids.

"Fuck," he groaned. "Your pussy's gonna break my fingers."

There was no response I could give. No biting remark. I had to focus on pulling air in through clenched teeth. He'd gotten me breathing so hard I'd come close to passing out. The hand slid away. His zipper rang out. The table shook as he climbed on it.

His voice was pure sex. "Here's the cock you asked for."

He didn't give me any rest. His fat dick impaled me in a single thrust. My mouth fell open, but no sound came out and my heart refused to work properly. It slammed in my chest just as fast as he slammed into me, and it burned so good.

His clothed body pressed to my naked one, and my nipples rubbed against the cotton of his t-shirt. I loved feeling his weight on me. Then he shifted, taking it away for a moment, and when his body pressed back down, it was warm skin on mine. He'd pushed his shirt up so we could have delicious contact.

The fingers of my unbound wrist flexed and curled back into a fist. I yearned to touch him, or to push my blindfold up so I could watch as he fucked me. Whimpers flowed from my mouth. Desperate, pathetic noises that only seemed to make his cock harder and his thrusts deeper.

"You feel so fucking good," I mumbled into the side of his neck. The flutters in my belly began once more, and I was quaking beneath him.

"You ready to come again?" His voice was corrupt.

My head bobbed up and down, nodding violently. One hand slipped beneath me, grabbing a handful of my ass and squeezing just to the edge of pain. He slammed his hips against me, driving his cock at a furious pace. "Then fucking do it."

I moaned as he shoved me over the edge into euphoria. Another of my screams filled the room, but this one was followed by his loud groan, and it set off a series of jerks from him. His cock pulsed inside me, one wave after another of heated bliss.

The tense muscles pressed against mine began to relax as he recovered from his orgasm. "Shit, our American sex is epic."

A short laugh fell out of me. "Our Japanese sex isn't a joke either."

"We should teach classes." He faked seriousness. "People could learn a lot from us."

"Right. Like how not to lie about your fiancée's car being yours." A finger tugged the blindfold off and I blinked at my vision suddenly being restored.

"It'll be mine eventually." His voice was heavy with meaning and his eyes glinted.

He was right in every sense. He pushed me, always getting his way in the end, and I loved every minute of it.

I loved it almost as much as I loved him.

Chapter NINE

EVIE

Processional music broadcasted softly from the small speaker in the cramped bridal room. It sounded tinny through the electronics, but I hoped it was beautiful for the guests sitting in the pews in the nave of the church. I was sure it was. Logan had picked the quartet himself.

Holy crap, it was really happening.

Logan's mom probably had the same thought. She'd been waiting for this day a long time. For years, everyone had assumed it'd be a lithe blonde marching down the aisle, not a brunette with thick thighs.

Why the hell was I thinking about his ex? I was a jittery mess, all nervous and excited and happy. I couldn't wait to see him, and I couldn't fucking wait to become his wife.

My gaze was glued to Payton, who held her bouquet of blue hydrangeas and white roses in one hand, and fiddled with the top of her bridesmaid dress. I'd let the girls pick their own, the only stipulation being that the dress was solid black. She'd chosen a strapless one that had a deep V notched in the center of the neckline, revealing her ample cleavage. By her standards, the dress was tame, but the priest was going to have a heart attack.

"Don't forget," I said to her. "Flowers up here." I held my bouquet up high over my chest. I need to crack a joke to distract from my nerves.

She smirked. "Are you insane? I'm not covering my best feature."

My father cleared his throat and Payton sobered, falling into line with the rest of my bridesmaids while we moved to the narthex. Only a set of double doors stood between Logan and me now. At the front of the line, Jamie disappeared through them with her arm linked to Logan's half-brother Garrett.

Payton had corrected Jamie at the rehearsal dinner last night when my coworker friend called me Evie. God, my best friend's little jealous streak was so funny. It's not like I'd demoted Payton's best friend status, but Jamie and I had become friends over the past year. Plus she had been awesome at helping plan the wedding on a budget. Thank God the Stones offered to pay for half of it. I was so blessed, and my family was grateful.

"Oh, no," I whispered to my father. "Don't you dare. If you start, I start, and I won't be able to stop." Tears stung and threatened to spill.

He wiped at his eyes and pinched the bridge of his nose. "I'm fine. I've got it together. It's just thirty feet." Since his tone was unsure, I stared up at the ceiling, desperate to drain the tears back.

Nick, Logan's brother, was the best man, but it made more sense for him to walk down the aisle with his wife Hilary, who was also a bridesmaid. Plus, this left Payton and Dominic to walk together. My heartbeat ratcheted up another level as Hilary and Nick disappeared into the church.

My knees were soft and uncooperative as Dominic stepped into view, offering his arm to my maid of honor.

"You look beautiful," he said as she threaded her hand through the crook of his elbow. "Oh, and you, Payton, you look nice, too."

She turned, flashed a grin back at me, and stepped off with Dominic.

"Thirty feet," my dad mumbled to himself, like he was trying to get pumped up.

My heart launched into my throat, blocking air as the song ended and the first strings of the wedding march began. I wasn't sure who was leaning on whom for support; both of us were shaking.

The doors swung open with the swell in the music, revealing the standing rows of friends and family who'd come to celebrate Logan's and my union. Every pair of eyes was on me, except for my father's. He was probably counting the steps as we moved forward.

No amount of visualization could have prepared me emotionally for this moment.

I'd seen Logan in a tuxedo before, and it had made me weak in the ovaries, but now he incinerated them. They didn't stand a chance against his perfect three-piece black suit, a formal black bow tied at his neck.

His focus was one hundred percent on me. There could be fireworks going off all around, we wouldn't have noticed. They couldn't compete with the fireworks between us anyway.

Logan's lips parted and shoulders lifted in a deep breath. Had I ever seen him this stunned before? My perfectly controlled man seemed to be struggling. The thoughts he held were loud on his face. He wanted to storm up the aisle and whirl me into his arms. He'd like to kiss me hard, and

ONE *more* RULE

probably fuck me harder.

Oh, God. I'd just thought about fucking while at church. I was going to hell.

The enormous skirt of my A-line dress swished as we ambled across the white aisle runner at a measured pace. My dad was rushing and I tensed my arm, trying to get him to slow down. There was so much to take in, I didn't want to miss any of it. Every step brought me closer to the man I loved, and I wanted to celebrate them each as a victory.

As the distance between us shortened, the depth in Logan's dark eyes grew. His expression filled with so much love, it was overwhelming. My bottom lip and chin trembled as I teetered right on the edge.

No, no, no . . . I did not want to cry. Why did people cry when they were happy? I fought to pull the corners of my mouth back into a smile.

"Ten, nine . . ."

Oh, good God, my father was literally counting under his breath. His stage fright was a welcomed distraction, and it was like a countdown to the moment I'd be with my groom.

"Five . . . four . . ." Logan straightened and his broad shoulders pulled back as he inched forward, as if he couldn't wait and wanted to meet me halfway.

"Three . . . two . . . one."

Logan's hand was extended to my father and the men shook. I leaned in, tilting my head as my dad kissed my cheek.

"I love you, Evelyn. Your mother and I are so happy for you." I closed my eyes, squeezing back fresh tears. "And I'm outta here."

My eyes popped open, and I choked on my laugh as my

dad scurried behind me, trying not to trip over my cathedral veil. My gaze turned back and found Logan's. His hand clasped mine and our fingers laced together. We turned toward the altar and went forward, together.

It was a blur after that. Readings, vows, and the rings. I slipped the silver band on Logan's left hand, and . . . yup, definitely going to hell. More impure thoughts at church. The band symbolizing his commitment to me was undeniably sexy. Our gazes and hands locked together.

The priest's baritone voice echoed in the vaulted ceilings. "You may now share your first kiss as husband and wife."

Even though I knew it was coming, the moment still caught me off guard. I wanted to lick my lips, which felt sticky from the long-lasting lipstick the makeup artist had applied this morning, yet Logan didn't give me time. As soon as he had the go-ahead, his fingertips glided over my cheek, gently drawing me in. His mouth lowered to mine and stole my breath. Soft, warm lips moved unhurried, taking as much time as he wanted, teasing me with a hint of tongue. I melted against his kiss as I always did. It was as shockingly good as it had been our first time that wild, out of control night outside the blindfold club.

No, wait, this was better. A million times better because he was my husband.

His kiss left me woozy, and I swayed when his hands retreated, my body mourning their absence. It was momentary, because he wrapped his hand around mine, holding me steady. His dark, intense eyes sparkled, helping further to pin me back in place.

The ceremony drew to a close, and it was impossible to

ONE *more* RULE

catch our breath. Pictures. The receiving line. The stretch limo that carried us with our bridal party to the Opulent Hotel where our reception would be.

We'd squeezed together to all fit in the limo, and with my enormous dress, I was practically sitting on Logan's lap.

"You look amazing, wife." He murmured it against the side of my neck, and I giggled.

"You look pretty amazing yourself, husband."

Being in the limo with him was a dangerous reminder of our evening last Saturday, and I shuddered with anticipation. Dinner, dancing, and then we'd be upstairs in the honeymoon suite, completely alone. No more closet or bathroom doors shielding his gorgeous body from my eyes, and no more self-imposed rules of keeping it in our pants.

By the time we arrived at the hotel, cocktail hour was nearly over. Payton hurried to bustle my dress in the handicapped stall of the bathroom while I slammed a bottle of water.

"There you are," Logan said when we emerged, as if we'd been in there for a century. "We need to line up for introductions." He threw a pointed look at Payton. "You're letting her fall behind schedule, McCreary."

She snatched a glass of white wine off a server's tray. "Yeah? I dare you to figure out the ribbons of her bustle faster than I did."

"The only thing I'm going to concern myself with Evie's dress," Logan said, "is how fast I can get her out of it."

I laughed, but it froze in my throat as my grandmother's head turned our direction. Shit! A light smile breezed on her lips, and she . . . oh my God. She winked.

Logan and I scarfed down our dinners so we could

spend as much time as possible mingling among the tables of our guests. I'd been to weddings where the bride and groom never once spoke to me and was determined not to have that happen at mine.

"I don't want to whine," I whispered to Logan as we began our first dance together. We were all alone on the dancefloor while our friends and family watched. "But my feet kind of hurt."

"Yeah? Mine too."

I had one hand on his chest and the other resting on the back of his neck as we swayed to the love song that filled the ballroom. Logan took my hand, held it away and led me through a turn under his arm. As I came back into his embrace, I stared up at him, wide-eyed. "What's this? It's not eight-grade dancing."

"My mom informed me I had to up my game. That's at least a tenth grade move I just gave you."

"Nice."

I was torn between not wanting the evening to end and my desire for it to be over so we could go upstairs. We laughed with our family, posed for pictures with friends, and ate a piece of our wedding cake.

My feet were aching and screaming for relief as the deejay played the final song of the night. Our crowd had thinned once the bar closed at eleven, and as soon as the song was over, the lights in the ballroom brightened. It had been an amazing day, but also exhausting.

Dominic's arms were tight around Payton's waist. "Logan," he said, his tone serious, "it's been a while for you. Let me know if you need any pointers for the wedding night."

"Thanks, Dominic. By the way, go fuck yourself."

ONE *more* RULE

Payton laughed. "He has me for that."

As soon as the elevator doors sealed us in alone together, Logan was on me. One warm hand splayed on the bare skin of my back while his other gripped my ass tightly, pressing me into him, crushing my dress. He held me into his kiss that was an assault on all fronts. My heart, mind, and body needed this man. My hand dove inside his tuxedo jacket, seeking the hardened muscles beneath the crisp dress shirt and three-button black vest.

"You have too many clothes on, boss."

"I'm fucking aware."

We hit our floor, he grabbed my hand, and tugged me down the hallway.

"Slow down," I gasped. "Not all of us are runners." He was dragging me along at break-neck speed.

"Is it faster if I carry you?"

I had no idea if he was kidding or not. We'd been together more than a year, and it wasn't any easier to tell. "I dunno, maybe."

A yelp escaped when his hands gripped my waist, lifting me, and not the sexy swept-up-into-his-arms kind, but the thrown-over-the-shoulder, caveman style kind of carry.

"Shit," he groaned. "Your skirt is huge." He banded an arm around my thighs, tucking the fabric out of his way so he could see, and took off. I bounced on his shoulder and the shorter, elbow-length veil I'd switched into for the reception hung down, trailing on the carpet.

"You don't like my dress?"

"I didn't say that. You took my breath away, Evie."

My heart thumped in my chest and my face warmed with a flush, but that also could have been the blood rushing to my head because I was upside-down.

"Hey, put me down before you hurt yourself." Although, if I were honest, I kind of liked this. His 'I have to have you now' attitude was seriously hot.

We were through the door and into the honeymoon suite. I couldn't see much, but the room was softly glowing with flickering light. His strong arms braced me as I slowly slid down his body until my feet were back on the ground. The veil was flipped over my head, and Logan lifted it, brushing it back.

"Are you thirsty? There's champagne."

"Oh?" I turned in his arms to face the room, ". . . my God."

A white, king-sized bed was against the left wall, decorated with a gold satin comforter and eggplant purple accent pillows. Mirrored, square lamps were perched on the nightstands. Everything was elegant and luxurious.

The back wall was like our apartment. Floor to ceiling glass with a view to die for, only this wasn't North Beach, it was the heart of the city, and the yellow-orange windows glowed in the night.

Also glowing were glass votive candles that lined just about every flat surface in the room. No lights were on, and it was breathtaking. I stood motionless as Logan went to the ice bucket and pulled out the bottle of champagne.

My desire for him was so strong I could taste it, but instead I remained still, watching him open the bottle and pour me a glass. I gestured to the room. "Did you arrange this?"

The only answer he gave me was a half-smile, but it confirmed he had. He held out the glass of champagne and I took it, letting my gaze fall to the other focal point in the room . . . the large Jacuzzi tub. It sat opposite the bed in a corner, the walls wrapped in mirror and the tile ledge around it was covered with more flickering candles.

It was romantic and seductive.

My gaze went back to him, starting at his feet and drifting upward over that sexy tuxedo, all the way until I could meet his eyes. Those chocolate brown eyes had been my undoing our first night together, and they were just as devastating now. Especially since they seemed to be filled with the same sordid thoughts he'd had then.

He poured another glass for himself but didn't take a sip. His intense focus was on me. "Lose the dress."

Chapter TEN

I swallowed thickly and smiled. I was eager, but . . . "I'm going to need your help."

Logan took a sip of his champagne and set it down, then shrugged out of his jacket. He tossed it on the chair nearby, and I'd learned he only disregarded his neat-freak status when he was impatient.

I loved how I did that to him.

"I'm happy to help, naughty girl."

I turned around and swept my veil over my shoulder so it wouldn't be in his way. "There's a hook at the top."

His tone was displeased. "And a shitload of buttons."

I smiled to myself. "Calm down, there's a hidden zipper."

Fingers drew a line where the fabric on my strapless dress stopped, tracing over my skin, and paused at the center to undo the tiny metal hook. Then, the zipper must have been discovered beneath the panel of buttons, because it began to drop, one tooth at a time.

I shivered as his lips floated over my shoulder, ghosting kisses. His hands were inside the back of my dress, pushing the bodice down, and sliding up over my belly. Making me tremble and insane with lust. My fingers fumbled in the small of my back to undo the knot holding my crinoline in place.

The cups were sewn in, so I wasn't wearing a bra, and my sigh of relief was loud when he palmed my breasts. I leaned into him, putting my back against his hardened chest. My eyes fell shut as I waited for his next move. I never knew what kind of sex I'd get with Logan. Did he want to make love tonight? Have a quick, hard fuck? Maybe both?

He enjoyed touching me, moving at an unhurried pace, but my body's response was too strong. I couldn't last much longer, so I shimmied out of the dress and my shoes. A tight noise came from behind.

"I like these." He ran a hand over the swell of my ass, admiring the blue panties I wore that had 'Mrs.' written in tiny rhinestones across the back.

"They were my 'something blue.'"

"Holy shit. It stands up on its own."

He was talking about my dress. "Yeah. No hanger required." The layers of stiff netting and boning supported the dress and kept it upright, defying gravity.

His fingers slipped under my arm and turned me to face him. His gaze traced each centimeter of my naked flesh like it was the first time he was seeing it, and he looked appreciative of the view. The only things I wore were the panties and the veil still attached at the base of my up-do. His expression shifted and grew more intense, mimicking one of a predator. This was the darkest version of Logan I only saw when he was overwhelmed with lust and losing his grip on control.

"I've missed these." Once again, his hands fondled my breasts, only this time he wasn't gentle. He moved on me urgently, forcing me backward until I slammed into the wall, but he didn't let up. Hands pinched at my already-tight nipples, making me ache while his mouth locked on mine. His tongue thrust deep, and I moaned.

But he stepped back abruptly and the heat of his body vanished, making my eyes fly open in surprise.

"Fuck." He ran a hand through his hair.

"Yes," I said, already breathless. "That's what we should do."

"We'll get to that, don't you worry, but I want to get in the tub."

I glanced at the large, deep Jacuzzi and gave him a dubious look. "You want to take a bath?"

"You mentioned your feet hurt."

They did, and now that I had it off, I was realizing just how heavy the dress had been. A bath with massaging jets and my gorgeous new husband wrapped around me suddenly sounded like the best idea ever.

While he ran the tap, I went to the mirror and began the process of removing my veil. I said it loudly over the rushing water. "There are a thousand pins inside my hair, just so you know."

"Awesome."

Movement from beside the tub stopped me mid-process. Logan was getting undressed and I wasn't about to miss the show. The vest was already open, and the tie hung loose around his neck. Sexy. Then, the shirt was unbuttoned and cufflinks undone. I gasped when he peeled one shoulder out, followed by the other, and dropped all of it to the floor in a heap.

I couldn't stop the grin at how he was breaking his own rules.

"What?" he said. "It's a rental."

"Okay, boss. I can pretend you're not going to pick all that up later because it's bothering you."

He smirked. His hands busied themselves undoing his pants, and it showed off his impressive upper body. All sinewy muscles flexing under his smooth, tan skin. The pants fell off his hips, slid down, and he kicked them away. The black socks were tugged off and added to his pile.

Witnessing Logan in only a pair of black boxer briefs set my body on fire. I freed the comb that the veil was attached to from my hair and, following his lead, I dropped it to the floor.

"Come here." It was a soft request from Logan, not a demand, and I went to him instantly. His hands swept over my skin, greedy to touch what he'd been denied. They plunged beneath the back of my panties, and he gripped a handful of flesh, driving me against his hard body.

"I love you," he whispered between kisses, which grew reckless and frantic, and it was impossible not to match his intensity.

"I love you so much," I answered back, clawing at his underwear.

It was a race to see who could get the other one naked first, but he won, of course. He lifted me up into his arms and stepped into the tub. A moment later he had the faucet shut off and the jets running, both of us sitting in the warm water. My back rested against his chest, while his strong arms held me, and his legs were wrapped around my waist.

There were tiny tugs at my hair. Was he . . .? I glanced over my shoulder and saw him set the bobby pin on the tile. Then, another. Shit, this man made everything sexy, even something as simple as helping me let my hair down. I grabbed his foot and pulled it into my lap, massaging the sole, and he issued a groan of approval.

We chatted about our morning apart, recapping our favorite moments from the day as he pulled the pins from my hair and I rubbed his tired feet. It wasn't the type of intimacy I thought we'd share the moments after we came into the honeymoon suite, but it was wonderful. I loved the quiet moments with him just as much as the steamy, intense ones.

"I think I got them all," he said. His fingertips drifted down my neck and he rubbed my shoulders as I combed my fingers through my hair, searching for any stragglers.

"Good . . . job," I moaned. His hands were magic.

"What would you say if I told you we should get out so I could fuck my wife senseless?"

"I'd say I like the sound of that."

"Hmm. I thought so."

The jets were shut off and the water gurgled as he lifted the drain stop. I'd barely finished toweling off when he yanked the plush fabric from my hands and threw it to the ground. His expression was pure sexual hunger, only intensified in the candlelight. A gentle shove, and I was sprawled out beneath him on the bed.

"Look at you. All fucking gorgeous and so fucking mine."

My lungs refused to work as he gripped his thick cock and stroked himself, his wedding band the only thing he wore. I couldn't control myself. My fingers flew to my clit, touching myself.

"Oh, shit, Logan. I need you."

He sank down to kneel and placed my knees on his shoulders. My body didn't know how to react. I loved when he went down on me, but I was greedy and impatient. "No,

ONE *more* RULE

please— God." Then his tongue was inside me, and thought was too difficult. "Yes, yes."

Velvety heat flicked on me, sending sparks radiating out and down my trembling legs. My moans were a mixture of satisfaction and whining, and they grew louder with each of Logan's careful manipulations. Fire seared deep inside, and I bucked off the bed, seizing his head in my hands.

"Make love to me," I cried. Every cell in me was quaking, and I worried I was going to vibrate apart. The only thing that could stop my uncontrollable trembling was if he brought us together.

The bed shifted as he launched to his feet, wiping his mouth with one hand and giving a final stroke to his rock-hard cock. He held himself steady and positioned himself right at the apex of my legs, rubbing the tip in my arousal.

"Green?" he teased.

"So fucking green. Please. Please."

He pushed inside and I wanted to cry at how good it felt. The stretch the first time he moved in me was like nothing else. My legs tightened around his waist.

"Fuck, Evie. You feel amazing. So wet and so perfect."

My eyes squeezed shut so I could better enjoy the sensations as he slid deep, all the way until I couldn't take him any further. My hands clutched at his chest and he gripped them, linking our fingers together so he could hold my hands flat against the sheets.

His thrusts were slow and calculating. Each one seemed to hit a new spot that was better than the last. His mouth roved over my lips, my neck, and my breasts. I swallowed back a moan as he increased his pace. Spots danced in front of my vision as the orgasm closed in.

"Yellow," I gasped.

I was sure I didn't need to tell him; he knew my body better than I did sometimes. He knew exactly how much I could take, how much I needed.

"Did you . . . hear me?" I said between pants. He hadn't eased up.

His voice and expression were authoritative. "I heard you."

I fought against his hold. He needed to slow his roll or I'd come, which usually made him come. "Fuck. I'm gonna . . . oh, red. Red!"

"No, Evie. You're not allowed." And then his mouth was on mine, sealing me off from asking permission to come. It wasn't a game we played while I'd imposed the rule, and with what he was doing to me, I'd forgotten all about it.

I turned my head away from him and my voice shook as I demanded it. "I need permission."

"For what?" He whispered it in my ear, his tone coy.

"Permission to come."

He sucked on the tender spot of my neck, just below my ear. He drove into me. This wasn't lovemaking. He was owning my body now, and I lifted my hips up off the mattress, eager to meet him.

"Okay, Mrs. Stone. You have my permission to come."

I let out a cry, or maybe a scream as it began. Sparks of pleasure burst, lifting me higher and higher, until I fell over the crest of bliss. My muscles tightened and strained against the sensations rolling through me. As the intensity of the orgasm began to fade, warmth washed from the tips of my toes upward.

"Fuck. Oh, fuck." Logan's curse words signaled the

ONE *more* RULE

trigger had been pulled on his release. His right hand abandoned mine, and scooped beneath my neck, cradling my head. "Open your eyes."

His damp forehead rested against mine and I followed his command. Oh my God. His fascinating eyes stared down into my soul as he shuddered. He came hard, and loudly. Every desperate gasp for breath was for me. The throbbing of his body inside mine . . . I'd never get enough of this. My connection to him was so strong, nothing could break it.

His skin, still damp from the bath, or perhaps slick with sweat, stuck to mine, but I didn't care. For a long while we lay on the bed kissing and touching, enjoying each other.

"Want to make a deal?" I whispered.

"I'm listening."

"You blow out all these candles and let me lie here, and I'll blow you when you're done."

He twisted his mouth into a knowing smile. "Right. I'm sure you won't be fast asleep when I get back here."

I put my hand on his jaw, brushing my thumb over his lips. "I didn't say when specifically I'd blow you."

"New rule, then. Promised oral sex must be delivered in a timely fashion."

I giggled. "No more rules, Logan."

He rose up on an elbow and brushed a lock of my hair out of my eyes, his face going serious. "One more rule. We say 'I love you' every night before we fall asleep."

It was something we already did, so I had no problem defining it this way. "Absolutely."

"Don't go breaking it, rule breaker." He faked a strict, harsh look.

"Never, boss. I love you."

"I love you too, Evie." He pressed his lips to mine in a kiss full of passion. "More than you can even imagine."

And since I knew how much I loved him, I could imagine a lot.

THANK YOU

To my husband. You're all the best parts of my heroes and then some.

To my editor Lori Whitwam for squeezing this project in. You always make me feel like such a rockstar whenever I get your emails.

To my beta readers Robin Bateman, Keyanna Butler, Joscelyn Freeman Fussell, Rebecca Nebel, and Nikki Terrill for your great feedback and comments. *"I think he should slap her pussy here..."*

To the fans of the Blindfold Club series (especially my Naughty Nymphs). Your support means the absolute world to me, and I can't thank you enough.

ABOUT THE AUTHOR

Nikki Sloane landed in graphic design after her careers as a waitress, a screenwriter, and a ballroom dance instructor fell through. For eight years she worked for a design firm in that extremely tall, black, and tiered building in Chicago that went through an unfortunate name change during her time there. Now she lives in Kentucky and manages a team of graphic artists. She is married and has two sons, writes both romantic suspense (under the name Karyn Lawrence) and dirty books, and couldn't be any happier.

Find her on the web: www.NikkiSloane.com

Contact her on Twitter: @AuthorNSloane

On Facebook: www.Facebook.com/NikkiSloaneAuthor

On Instagram: instagram.com/authornikkisloane

Send her an email: authornikkisloane@gmail.com

WHAT'S NEXT?

Book 4, titled "Three Dirty Secrets" is set to publish in January 2016. You'll learn more about Regan as she tangles with the sexy tattoo artist Silas, who's mentioned in book 3.

If you haven't read book 3, "Three Little Mistakes" it's already available as I wrote this novella out of sequence.

THREE *little* MISTAKES

I sell sex, sin, and pleasure, but it isn't just my business, it's my entire life. I get off on the power of controlling it all.

She's the one woman I can't have.

She threatens everything, and yet I can't stay away. There's a beautiful, sexual creature inside this timid girl that's desperate to claw its way out. I'm going to set it free, even if it brings my empire tumbling down.

I have to believe she'll be worth all the little mistakes I've made.

Made in United States
Orlando, FL
15 August 2023